"Good night, my lord." ... to the doorknob.

"Let your hair loose from now on," he said abruptly.

Her hand flew from the knob to where she hastily pinned locks hung in disarray around the nape of her neck. "Oh, sir! I couldn't. It wouldn't be at all proper."

"Perhaps not, but . . . please do it." His hand reached out and slowly brushed a tendril away from her cheek.

Jane nearly gasped aloud as his fingers, barely touching her skin, sent sparks throughout her whole being. As she breathed in, she was acutely aware of his scent, a mixture of bay rum, the faint spiciness of wine, and the earthy masculinity of exertion. She quickly averted her eyes to the floor, hoping that in that brief moment he hadn't read her desire for him to keep touching her.

His hand seemed to linger just an instant, then dropped to his side.

"Good night, Miss Langley," he said softly, as he turned and walked quickly down the hall.

The Defiant Governess

by

Andrea Pickens

A SIGNET BOOK

SIGNET
Published by the Penguin Group
Penguin Putnam Inc., 375 Hudson Street,
New York, New York 10014, U.S.A.
Penguin Books Ltd, 27 Wrights Lane,
London W8 5TZ, England
Penguin Books Australia Ltd, Ringwood,
Victoria, Australia
Penguin Books Canada Ltd, 10 Alcorn Avenue,
Toronto, Ontario, Canada M4V 3B2
Penguin Books (N.Z.) Ltd, 182–190 Wairau Road,
Auckland 10, New Zealand

Penguin Books Ltd, Registered Offices:
Harmondsworth, Middlesex, England

First published by Signet, an imprint of Dutton Signet,
a member of Penguin Putnam Inc.

First Printing, January, 1998
10 9 8 7 6 5 4 3 2 1

to Kevan,
my real life prince

Chapter One

The afternoon sunlight flooded into the drawing room, playing off the golden highlights of the Aubusson carpets, rich brocades, and gilt furniture, as well as the honey-colored curls of the young lady seated at the pianoforte. She had left off her music for the moment and sat staring out the soaring mullioned windows, her chin cupped in her hand. Outside, manicured lawns and formal gardens were already hinting at the lushness to come, acre upon acre stretching out to where the home woods of ancient elm and oak separated the imposing stone manor house from the vast expanse of the estate's farmland and forest.

But her gaze seemed to take in none of the details of the view before her. It certainly took no note of her own reflection in the leaded glass panes, one that showed a young lady of above average height, quite slender, with well-cut features that indicated a certain firmness of character. They were perhaps too strong to be called beautiful in the soft, conventional sense, but combined with the restless energy that radiated from her person they created a striking picture. Below the slightly furrowed brow were eyes of the deepest sapphire, cloudy for the moment. The purse of her firm, full lips also betrayed a sense that her thoughts were elsewhere, but then she quickly gave a shake of her shoulders, as if to banish whatever was bothering her.

With a slight frown she turned a page of the music and began to play again. The lilting notes that filled the room bespoke of a more than ordinary talent, even though the piece was a difficult one. As she came to a particularly complex movement her fingers flew over the ivory keys without a moment's hesitation—bold, fortissimo—and the effect was mesmerizing right until the very end when a wrong note rang out.

"Oh, damn," she muttered as she brushed a stray lock from her face.

"That will *never* do in Town, my dear Jane. You know very well it's not at all the thing for a lady of breeding to even *think* such a word."

Lady Jane Stanhope spun around, a guilty look on her face until she saw who had caught her. "Oh dear," she replied, trying to keep the smile off her lips. "I shall never take, shall I, Thomas, if I don't mend my outspoken ways."

Thomas, Viscount Mountfort, also struggled to suppress a grin. His features were as finely chiseled as those of his sister and because of their obvious closeness most people wondered if they were twins, though she was a year younger.

"Never," he agreed. "You're a complete hoyden, I fear." Not, he added to himself, that her more than occasional unladylike behavior had kept a bevy of the most eligible bachelors in London from dangling after her during her first Season. Hadn't she rejected the Earl of Havesham and the Marquess of . . .

"And I fear you have the right of it." She sighed, once again staring out through the leaded glass. This time the sunlight caught not just the richness of her hair and the gleaming blue of her eyes, but the stubborn thrust of her chin, a look Thomas knew all too well.

He moved quietly to her side and placed a hand on her

shoulder. "What's this? Feeling blue-deviled? I thought you were looking forward to another Season in Town."

"Oh, I suppose I am. It's just that, well . . ." How could she describe what she was feeling? She wasn't sure she herself understood it, let alone be able to put it in words. A sigh escaped her lips. "In Town there are so many constraints on a lady's behavior. I must act as if I care for nothing but the latest fashions and *ondits* when I make morning calls with Aunt Bella. Then at night there are all the boring gentlemen who look as if they have swallowed a frog if I express a real idea or opinion." She looked up at him to see if there was even a glimmer of understanding of what she was trying to say.

"But you have many admirers who enjoy your outspokenness, who think you are a True Original." It didn't hurt matters, he forbore to add, that she was the daughter of a duke and an heiress in the bargain.

"I don't want to be appreciated as an Original." Her tone had turned angry. "I want to be appreciated for . . . what I am, not—oh, never mind."

"Enough of this! You've been cooped up inside too long on such a lovely day that it's given you the megrims. I know just the thing. Would you care to match your Midnight against the new stallion I just bought at Tattersall's? He just arrived this morning. I warn you though, he's a prime one."

Jane jumped to her feet, eyes sparkling with the challenge. Though her brother was six feet tall she could almost look him in the eye, and her willowy form was bristling with indignation. "Oh, you don't truly think you can beat me!"

Thomas shrugged his broad shoulders, hardly wrinkling the impeccable cut of his coat. He stared nonchalantly at the tips of his well-polished Hessians, as if contemplating her statement. Secretly he was relieved that the storm he'd seen gathering on her brows had disappeared, to be replaced by her normally exuberant spirits. He waited another few moments in silence, just long enough to start her foot tapping impatiently on the carpet.

"Care to wager on it?" he drawled.

"A gold guinea!"

Her eyes were flashing bright as the named coin and with a start he realized how truly beautiful his sister was. Oh, it was not just her features, which were certainly lovely, but something else—a bewitching vitality. He sometimes worried that it ran too unchecked since both his widowed father and the entire household doted on her, but it was no wonder that so many of the most eligible bachelors, used to demure schoolroom misses, were intrigued. If her spiritedness sometimes crossed over the edge, he was sure that many of her hijinks were due to something other than true willfulness. He was aware that since her come-out last year the strictures on her behavior, especially in Town, had inexorably tightened. The escapades were her way of fighting back, of expressing her independence. With her keen mind she could have no illusions about how Society viewed her spirit. They meant to break it, to make her take the bit between her teeth. It was time she married and it was expected that she would fall into step like a demure mare, like all the other girls her age. How repugnant—and frightening— the idea must be to her, and how he admired her courage. He found himself echoing her opinion that it wasn't fair. But it was only a matter of time. Unlike a man, she had precious little choice. It was time she married and what man wouldn't want to control the reins? What rare man would accept an equal. . . .

"Well?" Her impatience pulled him out of his reverie.

"Done!" he answered, putting aside such serious musing for another time.

"Have Jem saddle the horses immediately. I won't be but a moment changing into my riding habit."

She spun and raced toward the grand stairway, nearly upending one of the parlor maids who was just coming out of the morning room. "Your pardon, Bertha," she cried, barely missing a step.

The maid gazed after her with the fond smile of a longtime retainer. Turning to Thomas she said, "Such spirit has Miss Jane."

Thomas nodded thoughtfully and wondered, not for the first time, in what hot water that spirit would eventually land his sister.

Two hours later the pair of them reentered the manor house, flushed with exertion and laughing uproariously over some private joke. One of the feathers of Jane's dashing little hat was sadly askew and she had taken off the entire creation, allowing a mass of curls to fall over the shoulders of her bottle green jacket, cut snugly in the latest military fashion. She shook her head to loosen the last of the hairpins. "Dear me, I'd better not let Sarah catch me looking like this—she'll ring a peal over me for not acting like a lady!"

"Oh fustian," jeered Thomas. "Since when has your maid or any of the servants done anything but indulge you at every turn? You have them all in your pocket, as well you know."

"That's not true," she protested. "James was quite cross with me . . . I think it was last month when I—" She paused and looked at him pensively. "Do you think I'm spoiled?"

Thomas thought for a moment. "I think there are times when you don't think of the consequences of your actions . . ."

"Excuse me, Miss Jane." Grimshaw, the family's butler ever since Jane could remember, had been standing patiently in the entrance hall, but as the friendly bantering between the two young people showed no signs of abating he felt obliged to interrupt.

"Oh, hello, Grimshaw. Forgive our bad manners for not greeting you earlier but Thomas and I have been engaged in a most important discussion." She turned to her brother. "Grimshaw most certainly doesn't indulge me." She looked back at the butler. "Do you, Grimshaw?"

Grimshaw gazed sternly at her, repressing the twitch at the corners of his mouth. "Certainly not, Miss Jane. Most improper it would be of me."

Jane grinned triumphantly. "There, you see!"

Thomas only rolled his eyes.

"Now, Miss Jane," said Grimshaw before the two younger members of the family could begin some other lark. "Your father asked that you see him in the library as soon as you returned."

Jane shot a questioning look at her brother. "I wonder what—you don't think he heard about me racing your curricle against Lord Cranston last week. Johnny was such a beast to insist no lady could drive prime cattle."

"Ssssh," hissed Thomas. "Let us hope not!"

"Lady Hepplestone was here earlier," added Grimshaw. His face was impassive but the slight sniff at the end of his words indicated his opinion of the person in question.

"Now what mischief has Aunt Bella been wreaking," muttered Jane. "Why she can't mind her own children's affairs and leave us in peace. Lord knows, with six to tend . . ."

"Six *boring* ones," interrupted Thomas.

"Six *hen-witted* ones," added Jane.

"Miss Jane!" The butler's stentorian tone filled the hall. "Your father said NOW!"

"Very well." She sighed. Tugging at her jacket and skirts to restore some semblance of neatness, she started toward the library. After a few steps she turned back to Thomas. "You don't think *she* heard about the curricle?"

"Lord help us both." He couldn't begin to imagine the set-down they both would receive if that was the case. Both stood in silent contemplation of such a ghastly thought until Grimshaw drew himself up to his full imperious height and pointed meaningfully down the hallway. Jane hurried away, leaving the butler to silently curse the meddlesome relative who always seemed to cause trouble for the young mistress of the house.

Her father was seated at his desk, head bent over some papers as Jane quietly entered the library. For a moment he was unaware of her presence and she found herself wondering why he had never remarried as she studied his handsome profile. His hair, though completely gray, was still thick, with a wavy curl that many young pinks of the *ton* spent hours in front of a mirror trying to achieve. His shoulders, broad and unbent with age, filled out the cut of his stylish coat as well as a younger man's. And the eyes studying the documents were still sharp and penetrating—sometimes too much so, she thought with a wry smile.

Henry James Sebastian Stanhope, the fifth Duke of Avanlea, looked up at his daughter. "Take a seat, Jane."

She knew immediately that something was very wrong. Even in his rare fits of temper there was always a certain look in his eyes, one acknowledging what they both knew: that she was the light of his life. Now suddenly it was missing, replaced by something she couldn't fathom, she who understood his moods better than anyone. Shaken and not knowing what else to do, she smiled as if unaware of the tension in the room. "I'm sorry to keep you waiting, Papa, but Thomas and I were—"

"Were racing—neck and leather I've no doubt— around the countryside like two . . . hellions," finished her father.

Racing, thought Jane. Then perhaps she was wrong and this was just about the curricle race. She cleared her throat. "I understand Aunt Bella was here earlier. If she told you about—"

"She told me nothing about any of your latest escapades. Just the usual dire warning that I have sadly mismanaged your upbringing."

"That's unfair," she cried. "Why can not Aunt Bella mind her own affairs! I have had a wonderful . . ." She paused. "Then why are you so upset with me? What have I done? Surely you cannot be angry because Thomas and I have had a nice gallop—why, we've been doing that for years."

"What have you done?" said her father in a quiet tone that belied the anger in his eyes. "Your aunt has informed me that Frederick Hawthorne asked your leave to pay his address to you and that you turned him down. Is this true?"

Jane was thoroughly perplexed. "Why, yes."

"May I ask why?"

"Because I don't care to marry him."

The duke leaned over the desk toward her. "You don't care to marry him," he repeated slowly. "And why is that? Is he a cruel man? A gamester? A rake? A simpleton?"

Jane shook her head. "You know he is none of those things. He's nice enough, but he lacks . . . a certain fire. He's rather priggish, if you must know, and I certainly don't feel about him the way one should about the man one is going to marry."

"And how is that? I should very much like to hear what a twenty-year-old miss scarcely out of the school-room has to say on such matters."

Stung by his words, Jane responded hotly. "I think one should feel love for one's future husband, not settle for a marriage of convenience that seems so popular among the *ton.*"

"What nonsense have I allowed you to fill your head with?" replied her father. "Is this the result of allowing you to study with Thomas and his tutor, learning French, the classics, history, and science, to read what you liked instead of insisting you be content with sewing, water-colors, and lessons on the pianoforte?" He shook his head. "Instead of a well-mannered, biddable daughter I have one with her head filled full of wild romantic notions."

"Biddable! You, of all people, have always encouraged me to think for myself, not to be a ninnyhammer like any one of Aunt Bella's daughters," cried Jane, her voice rising to the same pitch as his.

"Well, I have been wrong, I see. For an entire Season since your coming-out you have racketed around Town with your brother, getting into scrapes that should make a father blush. You have scorned any number of eligible young men—in short, you have indulged your own passions with nary a thought to your reputation or your future. That is going to change."

A silence descended upon the room. The cracking and hissing of the burning logs mirrored what both of them felt inside. Jane clasped her hands together so tightly that her nails dug into the skin. "Just what does that mean?" she asked.

"It means that *I* have given Frederick Hawthorne leave to pay his addresses to you. His father was a good friend of mine and I have known the young man since he was in leading strings. He has no vices, his estates are prosperous, his title is one of the oldest in the land, and you certainly cannot complain of his looks. I know he is considered quite a prize on the Marriage Mart. And he has character—enough backbone to deal with you, which unfortunately cannot be said for many. In short, I am convinced he will make you a very good husband."

Jane raised her chin defiantly and met his gaze in a clash of sapphire. "I shall never marry for a title or a handsome face. You cannot force me to altar."

"No, I cannot," he agreed. "But I think when you have had time to consider, you will come to your senses and agree that it is a reasonable course, one that will bring you happiness in the end. For you know," he added, softening his tone for the first time, "that is all that I want for you, Jane."

"How can you say such a thing?" She jumped to her feet, unable to rein in her emotions any longer. "You want to fob me off on a man I neither love nor even like above half! You of all people, who I know made a love match with Mama, and even today refuse to remarry because of her, despite all your mistresses . . ."

The slap lashed through the air like a whip, its crack stunning both of them into a shocked silence. Jane's hand flew to her face, as if it could erase the angry red marks of his fingers, and her father stared at his own hand as if it had acted on its own. The only sound between them was their own ragged breathing until the duke recovered his resolve.

"Never speak to your father thus, young lady. Your temper and your language only reinforce that I am doing the right thing, so listen carefully to me. There will be no Season in Town, no routs, no balls, no theater—nothing—until you see reason. From now on, you will not leave Avanlea until you leave it as the bride of the Duke of Branwell. And I am sending Thomas away to London tomorrow morning so you may contemplate in solitude the folly of your past behavior. It is to be hoped that in three weeks' time, the date for which I have invited Hawthorne to make an extended visit here, you will have come to your senses."

Jane made a horrified little gasp.

"And don't think to sweeten me up on this. I vow to you that I will not change my mind. It is time to grow up and be a dutiful daughter, and obey your father. You must trust that I know what is best for you."

Jane turned her head slightly so he would not see the tears welling up in her eyes. It was, after all, the only vestige of pride that she had left, not to fall at his feet in sobs. That her dear father had actually struck her, that he thought her shameless and a burden was almost too much to bear. But she refused to cry in front of him and show him how deeply he had wounded her.

"You have made yourself quite clear, sir," she replied tonelessly. "May I have your leave to go now?"

He nodded, restraining the urge to gather her in his arms and comfort her as he had done so many times in the past. She looked so miserable and forlorn as she turned to go that his heart gave a wrench. He prayed that his sister had been correct, that he was doing the right thing.

Jane raced blindly down the corridor, only vaguely aware of where she was or the sympathetic glances from the servants. She only knew that she had to make it to the front door, to the fresh air, to her horse.

Once mounted, with her stallion striding out in full gallop over the broad meadows of the estate, she finally gave way to her tears. They stung her face as the wind whipped at them. Her sobs mingled with the thudding of the hooves, creating a symphony of despair that she felt to her very heart. No one had a right to break her spirit, she told herself. No one! And yet she felt so alone, so small against the censure of her father, her family, the rules of Society. Was there anyone who would understand how she felt?

There was Nanna. Or, more properly, Miss Nancy Withers, who had come to Avanlea with the young slip of a girl who had been Jane's mother. Nanna, who had been her mother's nurse, who had followed her young mistress to serve as nurse to a new generation of children and who, by unspoken agreement of everyone in the household, had remained after the death of Jane's mother to keep a watchful eye on the two children, even long after they were out of the nursery.

It was to Nanna that a frightened and confused eight-year-old girl had run when the vast house suddenly fell silent and cold, then filled with a sea of black-clad adults who spoke in low voices to her papa. It was Nanna who had slowly coaxed a little sunshine back into all their lives, sharing picnics by the river, getting gloriously muddy hunting for polliwogs along its shallow banks, and even sparking the first laugh from her father by loosing a barnyard cat into the inner sanctum of Mrs. Greenwell's kitchen. Oh how they had had to stifle their merriment at the look on that august personage's face on seeing a muddy ball of fur plopped on an expanse of polished pine lapping cream from one of her spotless Staffordshire pitchers. Their father had hurried them from the door so as not to have the bad manners of laughing aloud, but once in his study they had all collapsed with mirth until tears rolled down their cheeks. That one shared moment had seemed to break the ice of his grief and once again he became the papa of old, sharing long rides around the estate and dinner together in the evenings.

It was Nanna, too, with whom she and Thomas had shared the intimate moments of growing up. The magic of a perfectly formed robin's egg, the tears at being too young to go to Town with Papa, the wonder of a first kiss.

Though she had retired to her own snug cottage on the estate last year, on Jane's first Season, declaring that now her little ones were truly grown up and didn't need her anymore, Jane rode over frequently to visit when she was home. Settling at Nanna's knee while Nanna knitted, just as she had as a little girl, she would regale her beloved old nurse with the latest gossip from London as well as confessing her and Thomas's latest escapades. Nanna chuckled and scolded, Jane looked contrite, and they both laughed and took comfort in the familiar warmth of each other's presence.

Jane burst through the door with a sob and without a word Nanna gathered her to her ample breast, thinking ruefully how little distance there was between eight and twenty.

"Come, come," she soothed, patting Jane's disheveled hair. "It's not like you to be such a watering pot. Dry your eyes while I fix some tea and then you'll tell me all about it."

She disengaged Jane's arms and handed her a linen hanky. "Now let me guess," she called as she put a kettle on the stove. "Lord Edgarton has proved a sad disappointment because the poem he's sent is not up to snuff with Byron's. Or is it Baron Haverill has refused to let you drive his matched grays, even though you are an infinitely better whip than he is?"

Jane couldn't help smiling in spite of her quivering lower lip. "Oh, Nanna, do you, too, think I am such a frivolous thing?"

"I'm quizzing you, love, as well you know. Now come sit down and tell your old Nanna what is wrong."

Jane hugged her cup close to her chest as if she needed its warmth. "So you see," she finished, "I am in an impossible situation!"

Nanna shook her head. "Your aunt has always been a meddlesome woman, always sparking no good. But I have been fearing your father would do something like this for some time now. I know he has been ill at ease about you. He has long worried that he hasn't provided you with the proper upbringing for a lady—it has been rather unconventional, you know—and he is quite concerned about making a good match for you. And you haven't helped allay his concerns, missy, with your behavior."

"But I will *not* be treated like . . . a prize mare, my merits and faults discussed by others, to be given, on careful consideration, to the highest bidder. I *won't*! I am a person with my own mind and I will not have my freedom taken away."

Nanna recognized the mulish tone in her former charge's voice and shot her a reproving look.

Jane bit her lip. "I'm sorry to sound like a fishwife, but when Thomas engages in pranks, he is called high-spirited—I am called shameful. It's not fair!"

"No, it isn't. It never has been," answered Nanna softly. "You know that well enough and it's something you must learn to accept."

"Must I?" asked Jane. "You, too, think I should accede to my father's demands and spend the rest of my life with a husband I care nothing for, a man who may order my entire existence exactly how he wishes?"

"Now, now." Nanna stroked Jane's hair. "I didn't say that. I just mean that it is time you admit that in your station in life you have certain options: You may remain on the shelf and care for your father in his dotage or become a doting spinster aunt to Thomas's future brood, hanging in his pocket and always making his wife feel a bit out of sorts with you—a life I assure you would not suit!"

"That's not the only option. I shall have an independent income when I come of age. I could set up my own house with a woman companion—you, Nanna. We could have our own establishment and do as we please."

Nanna shook her head. "Do you really think that would suit you either? No, you must marry. Certainly not Frederick Hawthorne if you don't wish it. But perhaps there is another young lord whom you are not adverse to. I'm sure your father would relent if you promised him you would settle down and apply yourself seriously to seeking a man you could be happy with."

"So instead of having my father sell me off, you would have me sell myself?" interrupted Jane bitterly. She tried to picture a face among the scores of eligible men who had ever shown a spark of true humor or hint of understanding when she attempted a heartfelt opinion. A void expanded inside her. "If these are the rules of my class, I wish them to the Devil! I never wish to marry! Would that I could change places with Mary Langley. No one bothers to try to force a farmer's daughter to marry against her will."

Nanna shook her head sadly. She loved Jane as a daughter and her heart went out to her in her misery. But she had seen this day coming for some time. With Jane's wealth and rank it had only been a matter of time before her independent streak of word and action would result in the reins being tightened. A part of her rebelled along with Jane at the injustice of it. Why, indeed, could a woman not be free to act as she chose? But she knew it was inevitable and it was better to help Jane realize and accept it.

"Little one, you are no longer a child but an adult, and must grow up and accept the responsibility of your station. Your life has changed." She noted the stubborn tilt of Jane's jaw, a look so familiar that she nearly smiled in spite of herself.

"But you always encouraged me to think that a woman had as keen a mind as a man. Why should I submit myself to the . . . tyranny of marriage? You never did!"

A cloud passed over Nanna's face. "That is true, my dear. But don't think I haven't missed things in life for it." She paused. "And don't think that your friend Mary has such a sweet life of it. Yes, she and Martin are in love and will be married. But until he found a position at Deerfield Manor he had no prospects and she was forced to look for a position, which as you know I helped her find. A good one, too, for it was as a governess to one small boy, the ward of a marquess who lives out of the country. I had heard through my sister, whose dear friend—well, it doesn't signify. But, mind you, she was going to work!"

"And control her own destiny," interrupted Jane.

"A fine destiny," said Nanna sternly. "In the employ of someone else. It's not such a fine life to work, my dear, though you shall never know it."

"Better than being leg-shackled. At least one can give an employer notice," retorted Jane.

"In any case, it is of no consequence for Mary. Martin is now upper footman to Lord Harbaugh and they will wed in three weeks' time. I'm sure she means to tell you herself tomorrow. She just stopped by here to give me the news and ask me to write her regrets that she is no longer able to take the position." Nanna motioned toward an envelope on her side table. "I have the letter right here. Would you be a dear and have your father frank it for me? I don't plan to walk into the village for another few days."

Jane slipped the letter into the pocket of her riding habit. "Of course."

Nanna gave her an affectionate hug. "Now, it's time for you to be off home or you'll be late for supper. Think about what I have said."

Jane spurred her horse into a smart canter. Her initial shock and despair had given way to an unyielding resolve. Just as everyone else was set on making her change, she was determined to do things on her own terms. No one would bridle her spirit! No one! Just what she would do, she still wasn't sure, but just the mere fact that she had made such a decision buoyed her spirits. She urged Midnight to greater speed, reveling in the feel of the wind in her hair and the raw energy of her mount. As she bent close over his mane, something jabbed her side and she remembered the letter in her pocket. Tugging at the reins, she slowed to a walk and took out the cream-colored envelope: *Mrs. R. Fairchild, Highwood, ——shire,* it said. After a moment's hesitation she broke the seal and took out the folded sheet of paper.

Dear Mrs. Fairchild,
I regret to inform you that the young lady I recom-

mended to you, Miss Mary Langley, will be unable to take up the post of governess to the Marquess of Say-brook's ward due to her forthcoming marriage. I know you expected her to arrive in a week's time, on March 21, and I am most sorry for any trouble this will cause you. Unfortunately I know of no other persons with the proper qualifications in this area that I might recommend to you. It is to be hoped that other of your acquaintances will be of more help to you.

> *Respectfully,*
> *Miss Nancy Withers*

Jane refolded the letter and put it back in her pocket. As Midnight continued his leisurely gait homeward, she patted it thoughtfully and a small smile crept to her lips, one of grim satisfaction.

Chapter Two

"Mary, I wish you joy, truly I do," said Jane as she hugged her childhood friend. Though Mary Langley was just the daughter of one of her father's tenant farmers they had become fast friends as little girls and had spent countless hours playing together. Nanna had encouraged the friendship, sensing that the motherless little girl needed such a companionship. She had even, with the duke's approval, seen to it that Mary had been included in some schooling, noting that as well as making the time more enjoyable for Jane and Thomas, it was providing the girl with a means of bettering her own life when she grew up. A well-educated girl could find work as a governess or companion, a step above being a farmer's wife.

Even as the girls grew up and the gap between their social status stretched more obviously between them, Jane never forgot her friend, and the two of them still spent time together, Mary listening raptly to the descriptions of balls, evening gowns and—heaven on heaven—the Assemblies at Almack's.

"Oh, Jane!" replied Mary. "I'm up in the boughs. I don't deserve to be so happy!" She shot her friend a guilty look. "I'm sorry about you and your father. Perhaps His Grace . . ."

"Nonsense." Jane smiled. "Let us not talk of my problems. I have faith that they will prove to be not insurmountable," she said obliquely. "Now, about Martin. I have always liked him. Tell me all about . . ." And she let her friend chatter on for the better part of half an hour.

"Oh," finished Mary, "I've been a prosy bore, haven't I, rattling on like this? I've kept you far too long."

"Not at all. I've thoroughly enjoyed myself."

Jane got up off the simple iron bedstead and wandered around the neat little whitewashed bedroom that Mary shared with a younger sister. A trunk was half packed in expectation of her coming move and one or two dresses lay draped over a wooden chair.

"Tell me, have you a few simple dresses—preferably gray or mouse brown—that you'd be willing to sell to me?"

Mary looked at her in astonishment. "Why, whatever for?"

Jane sat back on the bed and threw her arm around her friend's shoulders. "Do you promise not to tell a soul?"

Mary laughed, the scene so reminiscent of countless times before—Jane always instigating some mischief and herself a not-too unwilling partner. "Why is it that I sense I should leave the room right now?"

"There's really nothing for you to do," began Jane.

Mary rolled her eyes. "How many times have I heard that!"

"Truly. Just the dresses and your vow of silence."

"Go on. You know I can't say no to you. And besides, I'm dying of curiosity."

"You are engaged to be governess to the Marquess of Saybrook's ward . . ."

"Were," corrected Mary. "You know very well that Nanna has written my regrets."

"No indeed she hasn't. In fact tomorrow a letter is to be posted informing the housekeeper that Miss Langley will arrive on the twenty-first, as expected."

A look of horror spread across Mary's face as the import of Jane's words dawned on her. "You must be mad! Oh, it would never do. *You,* as a governess!"

"It suits perfectly. I am more than capable of teaching a seven-year-old his lessons. And the situation couldn't be more perfect. The marquess never visits his estate. The only ones there are the housekeeper and the servants, so there is not a chance of running into any house guests who might recognize me."

"I don't know." Mary shook her head doubtfully. "It doesn't seem right—you, a servant." She looked searchingly at her friend. "Have you really considered what it is like to work for someone?"

Jane returned her gaze. "I have thought about what it would be like to marry someone I don't care for. At least I may quit an employer. Besides, how truly awful can it be? The housekeeper is a friend of one of Nanna's acquaintances and is said to be a kindly woman. It is she I'll have to deal with. My biggest complaint will most likely be that things are too dull. I'll manage just fine, so please say you'll help."

Mary nodded reluctantly. "Of course I will. You know I'll not see you forced to act against your will. Now, I have a few gowns that will do. It's lucky that I'm a Long Meg, too, though fuller than you. And you'll need other things I'm sure you haven't thought of. You'll not have your abigail to take care of your needs, you know." She began to get in the spirit of things. "I have a list I made for myself. We shall pack a small trunk here. Martin can take it to Luddington next week and send it on by coach to Highwood."

"How clever. I had been wondering how to get my things out of the house," admitted Jane.

"Well, we'll manage." She eyed Jane's blond locks. "We'll have to do something about your hair."

"My hair!" exclaimed Jane.

"I'll give you a walnut leaf wash to dull its color. And spectacles. Yes, that will be a good touch."

It was Jane's turn to look surprised.

"No matter that it's only a housekeeper instead of the marquess. There will still be other servants and it doesn't do to be too . . . you know, attractive. Mamma has explained to me how lords may look upon a governess."

"Oh," whispered Jane. "I hadn't thought of that."

"And no doubt not a good many other practical things. We shall have to sit down and go over what is proper behavior . . ."

"Not you, too," muttered Jane.

"If you are going to pull this off, you cannot act like a duke's daughter," warned Mary.

"You're right of course. I'll be a quick study, never fear." She gave Mary a hug. "Thank you. You are the best of friends."

"Just see that this whole scheme doesn't land you in deeper suds than you are already in or I'll never forgive myself."

"Oh, don't worry. What possible consequences can come from a little harmless deception?"

Mary looked doubtful. How many times had she heard similar sentiments being uttered, in complete sincerity, at the start of some madcap adventure?

Late that night, after sitting through another dinner marked by the strained civility that had sprung up between her and her father, Jane dismissed her abigail, sat down at her writing desk, and took out a sheet of paper.

She unfolded Nanna's letter and copying the familiar looping script, began to write:

> *Dear Mrs. Fairchild,*
> *I am happy to inform you that Miss Jane Langley will arrive at Highwood on March 21, as expected. I trust she will prove satisfactory.*

Jane paused for a moment, then, with a mischievous gleam in her eye, added:

> *I assure you she is a very biddable and well-behaved young woman, even a trifle shy, and will give you no trouble at all.*

Dawn had not yet broken a few days later when a lone figure clad in a hooded cloak and carrying a worn valise and reticule slipped out of the kitchen door of Avanlea into the shadows of the shrubbery. She passed, like a ghostly specter, into the surrounding woods. The moon scudded in and out of clouds, offering little light by which to see among the tangle of underbrush and brambles, but Jane was not deterred by the thorns that caught at the rough wool of her garments. She quickly found the path that the gameskeeper used to patrol the upper reaches of the estate and hurried her pace even more. After perhaps a mile, she reached a broad meadow where she climbed over the stile and turned left, keeping herself close in the dark shadows of the surrounding stone wall. At the far corner she heard a soft whinny and was relieved to see a rough cart silhouetted against the sky, a solitary figure stroking the horse's head to keep it quiet. At the sound of her footsteps, the figure moved forward to take the valise and help her onto the open seat.

"Everything all right, miss?" whispered the figure.

"Yes. I'm sure no one saw me leave."

The figure grunted in reply and scrambled up beside her. "Well then, let's be on our way."

The cart bumped over the rough track as the person beside her twitched the reins, urging the horse to as great a speed as he dared. "I'm sorry for the discomfort, Miss Jane," he said. "It will get better when we reach the main road."

"It doesn't matter." Jane smiled as she reached over to pat the driver's arm. "And I can't thank you enough for your help, Martin. I shall never forget it."

Martin returned her smile gamely but she saw how nervous he was. "After all you have done for my Mary, 'tis the least we could do for you."

He looked back over his shoulder into the pale mist rising over the fields. "The stage arrives at Hinchley at half six and you should be safely away before any of your people are any the wiser. And hopefully no one will take notice of a simple farmer's wife—begging your pardon, miss." He tugged his own hat down low over his brow as he spoke.

"Do not be nervous, Martin. No one will know of your part in this, I swear. I promise you that you will not suffer for helping me—and Mary will tell you that I never break a promise."

"Oh, miss, it ain't the duke I'm worried about. 'Tis Mary that'll have my head if I don't get you away safely."

Jane laughed softly. "Well, put your mind at ease. All will go well. And now," she added as the cart turned onto the market road, "I think you may put us to a trot."

Martin did as she suggested, bucking up his own spirits at the calm assurance in her voice. They rode the rest of the way in silence, arriving at the staging inn with plenty of time to spare. Martin kept to the edge of the stables and reined in behind two other farmers' carts. There was just one other person awaiting the coach, a short heavy man dressed in a greasy coat, with two equally grubby burlap bags at his feet that moved in a most peculiar fashion. He blew into his stubby fingers to ward off the early morning chill and stamped impatiently in the dirt and chaff, sending up little clouds of debris with each smack of his worn boots.

Jane momentarily blanched at the idea of sharing a coach with such a person but then chided herself on such weakness of spirit. She had better get used to such things, she reminded herself—from now on she was no different from that man.

A sharp horn blast punctuated the stable sounds, announcing that the mail coach was fast approaching. Martin helped Jane down from the cart. She caught him about to bow his respects and threw her arm around his shoulder to forestall any such display.

"None of that, Martin," she whispered in his ear. "You must hug your wife good-bye and hope that her mother's illness passes quickly so she may return to you and the children." She noticed a faint blush spread across his cheeks.

"Miss Jane, I couldn't . . ." he began, but realizing she was right, he took her arm and walked toward where the mail coach had lumbered to a stop. Raising his voice he announced, "Now off with ye, Mary and here's hoping yer mother recovers soon." He winked broadly at the coachman. "'Course the children will miss ye, as will I."

He tossed the valise onto the roof of the coach and helped Jane into its dark interior, giving her a pat on the backside which would have sent her into a fit of giggles if her throat hadn't felt so constricted. She settled in between the greasy farmer and an older woman who was snoring loudly through an open mouth. The heat of their bodies and the musty smells of unwashed clothing and stale tobacco overwhelmed her senses. She closed her eyes to hide the shine of tears from anyone who might care to notice, hoping she might as easily close out her past life. It was but a small price to pay for her independence. That thought revived her sagging spirits—how many young ladies of Quality would have been corkbrained enough to consider going to work as a governess as freedom? Suppressing a small smile of irony she sank back against the seat and tried to sleep, telling herself not to think too much about what the coming days might bring.

The coachman knocked on the massive oak door, and from behind his shoulder Jane saw it swing open slowly to reveal an elderly butler, stooped yet still tall and attired in somber clothes.

"Miss Langley has arrived."

"Thank you, William. You may put her valise in the hallway."

Jane was left alone to face the butler. She searched his visage for any reaction to her arrival, but his features were impassive, as was his voice when he finally spoke to her.

"We have been expecting your arrival, Miss Langley. Come inside while I inform Mrs. Fairchild that you are here."

Jane stepped into a capacious entry hall whose polished oak floors and handsome carved paneling and furniture were redolent of beeswax and lemon oil. As she glanced through the open morning room door at the elegant drapes and carpets, she noted that though the master of the house may rarely show his face, the estate was being managed by someone who cared.

Her thoughts were interrupted by the jangling of keys, then the opening of a door. She turned toward the sound to meet the gaze of a stout woman with rather plain features, no taller than Jane's chin. Her gray hair was pulled back in a simple bun, though some stray strands had loosened themselves from under the white mobcap, giving her the air of someone in perpetual motion. From her ample waist hung the source of the noise, a huge iron ring with all manner of keys silhouetted against a pristine starched apron.

Jane quickly remembered Mary's admonitions about proper behavior and bobbed a graceful curtsy. The lady nodded in approval, Jane noted with relief, and the broad smile that lit up her face was warm and reassuring.

"Welcome to Highwood, Miss Langley. I am Mrs. Fairchild and I manage the household in the marquess's absence. I'm sure you must be exhausted after your journey—I myself cannot abide spending a full day in a coach, I don't know how you managed—so let me show you to your room. When you have refreshed yourself, I hope you will come share a cup of tea and some cakes that Cook has made up for us and then we can have a chat about your duties here, shall we?"

"Why that would . . . be very nice," managed Jane. Silently she gave thanks to her good fortune. The woman's friendly words as well as looks boded well for the future.

She was led up the imposing main staircase, feeling quite small under the stern gazes of the marquess's antecedents. Somehow she felt they were staring at her accusingly, as if they saw through her charade. Swallowing hard, she dropped her eyes to the polished treads. Mindful of Mary's description of life in service, Jane fully expected to continue up, into the attic rooms and then be shown a back stairway, the one she would be expected to use from now on. Instead Mrs. Fairchild stopped on the second floor and led her down a corridor to the right.

"I've put you near the schoolroom and Master Peter's room. I hope you'll find it agreeable," she said as she threw open the door to a small room flooded with sunlight and simply decorated in blue-sprigged chintz.

Jane was confused. "Oh, how nice," she exclaimed, taking in the polished pine dresser and armoire arranged to one side of a simple painted bedstead. "Are you sure this is for me?" she blurted out. "Surely this isn't a servant's room?"

Mrs. Fairchild smiled again. "We want you to be happy here." As she said those words, Jane noticed a slight cloud pass over her face, but just as suddenly it was gone. "I've had Polly bring you a pitcher of water to freshen up with. When you are ready, come back down the same way we came up and ask Glavin—he is that imposing figure you met by the door, but I assure he is not such a dragon as he appears—to bring you into the drawing room. Is there anything else you need?"

Jane shook her head, and when Mrs. Fairchild had closed the door, she sank onto the bed, her head in a whirl. She knew she should consider herself more than fortunate in having landed in such a seemingly agreeable position—she sensed that she and Mrs. Fairchild would rub along very nicely together. But now that she had finally arrived and was sitting in a modest little room with none of her familiar things or faces around her, the enormity of what she had done finally overwhelmed her. She had to fight back tears as she remembered the two nights at an inn, having to take her supper in the common taproom rather than a private parlor, having to endure the leers and comments of the men as she made her way to the tiny room consigned to a female traveling alone, a room where the sheets were suspect and the floor unswept.

She got up and splashed some water on her face, then regarded her own reflection in the small mirror above the washstand. Did her chin really have a defiant tilt? Did her eyes truly storm like an angry sea when she felt passionately about something? Though Thomas had teased her well enough on those counts, she couldn't see it herself. She only saw a stranger in the glass, a plain, bespectacled young woman dressed in a Quakerish gown of brown muslin, with mousy hair drawn into a severe bun. And the woman looked scared. After staring at her own image for a number of moments, she straightened her shoulders, the look of apprehension replaced by one of resolve. No, she vowed, she wouldn't be cowed that easily. Her pride wouldn't allow her to give up so soon and return home to accede to her father's dictates. No, she would meet the challenge.

She dried her hands and proceeded downstairs.

Glavin showed her into an elegant drawing room which, like the rest of the rooms she had seen, was decorated with exquisite yet understated taste. She was about to comment on the furnishing when she suddenly realized she shouldn't be cognizant of such things. So swallowing her words, she silently took a seat on the couch where Mrs. Fairchild had motioned for her to sit and folded her hands primly in her lap.

Mrs. Fairchild busied herself with pouring two cups of tea, and it was only after she had passed one of them to Jane and had liberally sugared the other one for herself that she spoke.

"I'm sure you are anxious to hear of your duties here at Highwood, and to meet your charge." She paused to take a sip from her cup while Jane dared not lift hers for fear that her hands would shake. "You will be expected to teach Peter his letters, history, geography, and—you do speak French, do you not?"

Jane nodded.

"And French. You may decide the hours of your schoolroom, but you shall be expected to look after him during the rest of the day as well—Cook has threatened to give notice if another gooseberry tart is knocked from the windowsill or if spiders keep appearing in the cream jug."

Jane had visions of an incorrigible little monster and her face must have betrayed her thoughts for Mrs. Fairchild quickly added, "Not that he is a naughty child, for indeed he is not. It's just that he is . . . well, I think he is lonely. The family nurse was forced by her health to retire two years ago and since then . . . It is very quiet around here, Miss Langley, as I trust you will soon discover. It is perhaps not an ideal place for a child to grow up, with no family . . ." She stopped abruptly.

"Did he not have a previous governess?" inquired Jane.

"She did not get along with children."

Jane wondered exactly what that enigmatic statement meant. "I hope I shall manage better," was all she could think of to reply.

There was a moment of silence while once again Mrs. Fairchild sipped her tea in a thoughtful manner. "I shall be frank with you, Miss Langley," she said, looking at Jane with a penetrating gaze. "The last governess was dismissed because I discovered her beating Peter."

"How awful! A child!" exclaimed Jane, unable to keep from speaking out.

"Yes, I thought so, too. And so I have gone to great pains to discover a suitable person to come to Highwood, someone I hope will stay for some time. I like you, Miss Langley, from what little I've seen of you. I trust you will be a good and kind companion to Master Peter." Again, a troubled look clouded her face for a moment. "And now, I think you should meet your charge."

She rang the bell that was sitting on the side table. Almost immediately the door swung open and Glavin ushered in a young boy who seemed pathetically small in contrast to the tall, bony butler.

"Come, Peter." Mrs. Fairchild smiled. "Make your greetings to Miss Langley. She is to be your new governess."

Jane watched the boy approach the couch warily, a pair of sea green eyes studying her intently from under a tousled mass of dark curls. They betrayed a mixture of trepidation and defiance. He ducked a quick bow, but then sidled close to the housekeeper, practically hiding behind her ample form.

"Not, now," Mrs. Fairchild gently chided. "Miss Langley will think you sadly lacking in manners if you don't greet her properly."

"Welcome to Highwood, Miss Langley." The words were mumbled and the eyes were now studying the tips of his shoes.

"Hello, Peter," replied Jane, essaying her warmest smile. Indeed, it wasn't difficult, for her heart had immediately gone out to the frail-looking child before her. In fact, the look in her eyes would have caused her brother much apprehension, for he would have recognized the beginnings of what he referred to as one of "Jane's crusades." Jane felt he exaggerated. Just because she was always the one to rescue a stray animal or lecture a tenant on the cruelty of beating a tired farm horse didn't mean anything other than that she disliked seeing the weak or helpless being taken advantage of. And though she admitted that no other female of her age or rank had shocked the drawing rooms of London by speaking out on the plight of juvenile chimney sweeps, she didn't think that made her a crusader, just a concerned individual.

"Won't you join me in having a cake? They are very delicious." She held the plate out toward him.

Peter looked sideways at Mrs. Fairchild, who nodded encouragingly. Then, a fondness for sweets overcoming his shyness, he tentatively reached out and chose a sugared walnut cake.

"Those are my favorite, too," said Jane in a confidential tone. "I particularly dislike gooseberry tarts because they have a nasty habit of falling off windowsills."

The green eyes momentarily widened, then she was rewarded with the merest glimmer of a smile before the pastry disappeared into Peter's mouth.

Jane turned to Mrs. Fairchild. "Perhaps Peter could show me around. I daresay I've kept you long enough from your duties, but I would like to see the schoolroom as well as the rest of the house so I may begin to learn my way around."

The housekeeper nodded in approval of the plan, adding a grateful smile of thanks. "What a splendid idea. Peter, why don't you start upstairs with the schoolroom." She rose and picked up the tea tray herself. "I should like it if you would dine with me tonight. At six, if you please." With that, she bustled out of the room.

"Shall we start?" asked Jane gently. "Or would you like another cake?"

Peter shook his head. His gaze had returned to the floor and without looking up he turned around. "Follow me . . . if you please," he mumbled.

The heavy door presented a bit of a problem. Even using both hands, Peter found it difficult to budge, but Jane let him manage. With a shove of his shoulder he made it swing open.

"Thank you, sir," She smiled as he held it open for her.

He didn't answer but moved ahead of her, leading the way back up the ornate stairway and past her own room. From behind she was able to study him more closely. He was a delicate child, with narrow shoulders which were now tight with apprehension. And yet he moved with a catlike grace unusual in one his age—Mrs. Fairchild had said he was seven, but he looked even younger. Perhaps, she mused, it was because his features were so finely chiseled, for in fact he was a beautiful child. Or perhaps it was because he looked so vulnerable. . . .

Her thoughts were interrupted by their arrival at the schoolroom. Peter dutifully opened the door and stepped aside for her to enter. It had an air of familiarity to it, the pine desks scarred by generations of pupils, the slates, the bookshelves crammed with dog-eared volumes, the globe on its varnished stand, the smell of paper, ink, and chalk. She felt a quick pang of homesickness as she looked around.

"What a nice room. Tell me, Peter, do you know your letters?"

The boy nodded.

"And can you do sums?"

He hesitated, then nodded again.

"Good, though I think you probably dislike it as much as I did. She smiled, hoping for some response from the boy, but he still remained stone-faced. "Well" she went on, "then we may start with some history and geography."

Jane wandered to the governess's desk and absently picked up a ruler that lay there. The boy instinctively flinched. She put it down nonchalantly, as if she hadn't noticed his reaction, and she felt a hot surge of anger to-

ward the guardian who could be so neglectful of his
ward.

"And of course we will learn harder sums and read the
works of famous authors." She stopped by the tall
shelves and looked at the spines of the leather-bound
books. There was a set of Scott's novels and Jane
couldn't hold back her enthusiasm. "Oh, these are wonderful books!" Impulsively she turned to the boy.
"Would you like me to read *Ivanhoe* to you?"

Peter looked at her in surprise. "I don't know," he finally answered.

"Has no one ever read to you?"

He shook his head. But then a moment later he said,
"My mother did . . . I think."

"Why don't we try it tonight and see if you like it. We
can read one chapter tonight at bedtime. What say you?"

He shrugged his small shoulders in a birdlike movement. "Okay."

Birdlike and vulnerable, she thought. It would take a
lot of patience to win his trust, but one look at those
wary, sea foam eyes told her it would be worth the effort
to bring some warmth to the life of a very lonely little
boy.

"We shall begin our studies tomorrow, but perhaps
you wouldn't mind showing me some more of the house
right now? Would you do that?"

"Okay." Then he corrected himself. "Yes, Miss Langley."

Jane bent down close to him. "Perhaps you might call
me Miss Jane. It sounds ever so much more friendly, and
I do hope we will be friends." She didn't wait for him to
respond but went on in a confidential tone. "One other
thing. This is such a big house that I find it rather frightening. Would you mind holding my hand as you show
me about?"

She reached out her own hand. He stared at it, then slowly placed his own palm within hers.

"Follow me."

Peter showed her the various rooms in the east wing, including the portrait gallery where Jane managed to coax the first tentative smiles from her young charge with funny comments on the dress or expressions of some dusty, long-gone ancestor. They were about to descend the main staircase when Peter pointed to the other wing. He was now putting more than two words together at a time, something Jane hailed as a major victory.

"That is where my uncle's rooms are."

She was surprised—from all that she knew, she had surmised that his guardian was elderly. But then she realized that he must be using the term loosely. Great uncle, no doubt.

"Your uncle is your guardian?"

He nodded.

"Is he very old?"

The boy nodded again.

Just as she thought. "And where is he?"

"I think he is . . . abroad," he answered vaguely.

Now that Bonaparte was safely tucked away on Elba, the rich and idle may play on the Continent again, she thought grimly, no matter what their responsibilities at home.

"When was the last time you saw him?"

Peter thought for a bit. "A year, I think."

"Well, perhaps he will visit again soon," she said, thinking that naturally the boy must miss his only family. And if he does, she added to herself, she would let him know exactly what she thought of his behavior. Then she realized that of course she wouldn't. She couldn't.

The boy immediately stiffened and said nothing.

Jane made another mental note. The boy didn't care for his guardian, or maybe it was that he was afraid of him. Did the man beat him, too? Was he one of those monsters who enjoyed hurting some defenseless thing? She vowed to learn more of the Marquess of Saybrook from Mrs. Fairchild, though of course she would have to be very circumspect. The lady was a relation, after all— though a distant poor one—and as such would be loath to speak ill of him, especially to a stranger. But Jane was determined to find out just what was going on here.

As she descended the stairs, she realized that for the first time in days she felt almost gay. She had a challenge, and there was nothing like that to buck up her spirits. Lord Saybrook had best beware, she vowed to herself. He may have bullied a small child in the past, but if he showed his face here now, he would have to deal with her.

Chapter Three

Over the next weeks a pattern to their days emerged. After breakfast in the morning room—which Jane insisted Peter eat along with herself and sometimes Mrs. Fairchild, rather than alone in his room as had been the habit—they would repair to the schoolroom for the rest of the morning. The lessons were gratifying for both of them, for Jane found her pupil had a quickness of mind and inquisitive nature that made learning easy for him. And she noticed that some of the wariness began to fade in the enthusiasm of reading a certain passage aloud or of adding a column of numbers correctly.

Afternoons were spent exploring the vast gardens and home woods beyond the manor house. Jane found a spot she particularly liked, a stone bench protected by a yew hedge that overlooked a small pond. Sometimes they would come with a book for Peter to practice reading aloud. Watching him giggle over a long and funny-sounding word, she suddenly felt a glow inside, that she could bring a touch of happiness to the child. Why, she realized with a start, she had been so concerned with the boy that she hadn't had time to miss her other life at all.

One day, after finishing a passage of Shakespeare, the sun was still bright and warm so Jane suggested they visit the stables, one of the few places they had not yet visited. She had been dying to see what manner of horses the marquess kept but had held her impatience in check, knowing full well that it wasn't expected in a governess. It was most difficult. More than once in her walks with Peter she had found herself longing to be able to gallop along the rolling fields and paths she saw.

The boy's reaction shocked her.

His face took on a mulish look and he jammed his hands in his pockets. "I won't go," he announced. "I *hate* horses."

"Why, Peter!" exclaimed Jane in disbelief. "I thought all boys were mad for horses. Don't you like to ride?"

He shook his head doggedly. "I hate it."

She reached over and gathered him into her lap. She had noticed that he wasn't at all used to being touched or hugged, and even though he wouldn't admit it, he seemed to like it very much.

"Now why is that?" she asked gently.

Peter didn't answer her.

"Did a horse hurt you?"

There was another pause until finally he blurted out, "A horse killed my mama. And my papa."

Jane pulled him closer while making a note to ask Mrs. Fairchild what had happened. "Oh, how terrible, Peter. I'm so sorry. But it must have been a terrible accident—horses don't mean any harm. They are quite fun, actually. Would you at least walk there with me so I can see them?"

Peter stayed pressed to her chest. "Uncle Edward thinks I'm a very poor-spirited boy not to want to ride," he said, fighting back tears.

Once again, Jane felt a wave of anger toward the callous guardian who was too insensitive to understand the boy's natural fear for what it was and help him overcome it.

"Well, I think your uncle is a complete gudgeon," she snapped. "Of course you don't like horses—I wouldn't either, unless someone took the time to show me they aren't all bad."

Peter looked at her in surprise and a bit of awe as she spoke. Then in a small voice he said, "You wouldn't?"

"No. But I'll show you some very special tricks for making them your friends, if you like. Maybe you'll change your mind. What do you think?"

He looked at her doubtfully.

"You don't have to do anything you don't want to, and I will certainly not think you poor-spirited. In fact I think you'd be very, very brave to even take a look at them."

He put his small hand in hers. "All right. If you stay with me."

The stables were an impressive set of buildings arranged around a central courtyard. To Jane's experienced eye it was obvious that they were well tended by someone who knew a thing or two about horses. There wasn't much activity at that time of the afternoon. A few nickers were heard from the horses inside their stalls and a stableboy could be heard whistling as he swept out the tack room. In an adjoining paddock, one lone horse stood placidly by the fence, twitching at the spring flies with its tail and browsing for bits of hay in the dirt.

Jane was relieved to see it was an old mare, one whose disposition was likely to be as peaceful as it appeared. She stopped, already sensing Peter's tenseness, and felt in the pocket of her gown for the apple she had saved from lunch. She took it out, along with a small penknife, and carefully cut it into quarters. She kept one out and put the rest back in her pocket.

"I'm going to make friends with this old mare," she said. "One bite of this apple and she'll look forward to seeing me again! Why don't you stay here and watch."

She walked toward the fence, holding the apple outstretched in her hand. The mare pricked her ears at the scent of food and gave a little whoosh of breath as she sidled right up against the rails. When Jane reached her, she eagerly gobbled the treat as Jane stroked the white blaze on her nose and tickled her behind the ears.

"Would you like to give her a piece? Her mouth feels like velvet rubbing against your palm."

Peter hesitated as he eyed the animal with some trepidation.

"It's quite all right if you'd rather not. She is rather big, isn't she? But she's also very friendly, as you can see."

The horse was now snuffling Jane's cheek and she couldn't help laughing at the tickling sensation.

That seemed to reassure the boy and he took a few tentative steps toward them. "You'll stay right beside me?"

"Of course I will."

That settled it. He came right to Jane's side, shying back a little as the mare poked her nose inquisitively down toward him.

"Hold the apple flat in your hand, like this," said Jane as she placed a slice in his palm. "Then reach out so she can see it." She put her hand on his shoulder to encourage him as he slowly lifted his hand. The horse dipped her head and gently took the proffered fruit between her lips.

"OOOOhhhhh," exclaimed Peter, jumping back. "It . . . tickled!"

"It does, doesn't it," Jane answered. "Do you want to try it again?"

Peter took another piece and this time he didn't flinch when the mare took the treat. He even rubbed the tip of her nose as she chewed contentedly.

"It's very soft," he murmured.

"If I lift you up, you could scratch her ears."

"Okay."

Jane gathered him up and held him steady on one of the rails so he could reach the mare's neck and head. He patted her forehead and ran his fingers through her mane. The mare turned and nuzzled his cheek.

"You see." Jane laughed. "She likes you!"

The boy smiled broadly.

"And you know what horses like even more than apples?" she added in a low voice. "Carrots and lumps of sugar."

"Do you think we could get some from Cook for tomorrow?" asked Peter, his eyes shining.

"I think that can be arranged. But now I think we had best get back before we are late for supper."

That night after she had read to Peter from *Ivanhoe* and put out his candle for the night, Jane went downstairs to where Mrs. Fairchild was knitting in the drawing room. She sat down and began to roll some of the loose skeins of wool in the work basket into neat balls. Mrs. Fairchild looked up from her work with a smile. "Why thank you, Miss Jane." She, like all the rest of the servants, had copied Peter in calling her thus. "It fits," Cook had announced with her characteristic forthrightness. "Miss Langley is much too stiff-necked for a nice, unpretentious lass like you."

Jane returned the housekeeper's smile. "I was wondering about something Peter said this afternoon," she began. "He told me that both his mother and father were killed by horses. I don't mean to pry in family history, but do you know what happened?"

Mrs. Fairchild's needles stopped clicking in midstitch. When she looked up, her face was pinched and drained of color.

"It was a terrible thing, it was." Her voice was low, almost a whisper. "The two of them were so gay, so lively. Henry warned them not to ride over the west bridge that afternoon, that the timbers had been loosened by the storm. But apparently they didn't heed him. They started racing each other. He tried to call to them—they reached the bridge together, urging their horses on. They were neck and neck in the middle of it when it gave way. The river was surging from the storm . . . Their bodies weren't found for two days. Their feet were still tangled in the stirrups." She shook her head repeatedly as if she could banish the whole incident. "And Mr. Edward's reaction . . . I . . . I still find it impossible to speak of. After all the other pain the family has had to endure . . ."

Jane lowered her eyes. She wished she could probe further and ask just what relation Peter's mother was to the elusive marquess, just what other "pain" it was Mrs. Fairchild spoke of. But she sensed the older woman could not be pressed anymore.

"I'm sorry to have brought back such terrible memories."

"You didn't know," replied Mrs. Fairchild. She continued her knitting, but after several exclamations of dismay at dropping a stitch, she placed the whole thing in her basket. "Forgive me if I retire early tonight. I find I am quite tired."

She looked tired, thought Jane as the other woman hurried from the room. Tired and what was it—sad, perhaps. Most of the time she was so open and warm, yet other times Jane sensed there was a shadow over her and this house. Jane shook her head as she picked up the book she was reading. She would keep trying to figure it out.

The next day, after lessons, Peter asked if they might get carrots and sugar from the kitchen and visit the stables again. Jane quickly acquiesced, glad to see the boy had lost none of his enthusiasm from the previous day. Indeed, when they spotted the mare—in much the same place as before—Peter let go of her hand and ran to the fence all by himself. Climbing to the top rail, he patted the horse's nose with confidence while feeding it the treats.

"Oh look, Miss Jane," he called as she approached. "She has eaten a whole carrot in one bite!"

"I told you," replied Jane. "I see we shall have to bring more on our next visit."

Peter was happily scratching at the horse's ears while it snuffled at his jacket. He grinned. "I think she smells the sugar in my pocket."

"Clever animal!"

Jane watched as the boy became engrossed in letting the animal gently mouthe the lumps of sugar from his hand. All fear and wariness had disappeared and she saw only the buoyant enthusiasm that she felt a seven-year-old should have. She let him manage by himself for a few more minutes then went and leaned on the fence next to him, basking in the innocent delight radiating from his face.

"All gone," he announced to the horse, holding up both hands for inspection. "I'll bring more tomorrow." He turned to Jane. "Can we, please?"

"Of course." She gazed out past the paddock toward the copse of oak and pastures beyond. "You know, when I was little we had . . . horses around and I used to love to ride through the fields and woods. There must be any number of wonderful things to explore around Highwood. Would you like to do that?"

Some of the light went out of Peter's face. "I can't ride," he answered, looking crestfallen, his hands clenched on the top rail. "I'm afraid."

"Yes, and yesterday you couldn't feed a horse."

She saw that he was mulling over her words and when he looked at her there was a touch of hope in his eyes.

"You can't ride, not because you're afraid, but because someone didn't teach you properly," she continued. "We're all afraid when we start—after all, they are such big creatures. But we get over it and then it is great fun, I assure you. Just like feeding this mare."

Peter hesitated. "Uncle Edward would be very pleased."

She had been wrong on one thing, she noted. The boy didn't dislike his guardian, he was in awe of him and craved his regard. Again she felt a surge of dislike for the man. Well, whether it made any difference to *him* or not, she was determined to help Peter overcome his fear.

"Yes, I'm sure he would, but even more importantly, *you* would like it. Do you want me to teach you?"

He nodded vigorously.

"All right then, let's go make arrangements with the head groom. We'll start tomorrow."

Henry, the head groom, agreed enthusiastically when the plan was broached to him.

"A very good idea, miss. It's time for the lad to get himself on a horse. But begging your pardon, miss, can you . . . handle a mount?"

"Oh yes indeed. I have been around horses all my life."

"Well," said Henry slowly, "I'd best see how you hold your seat afore trusting the young master to your care."

"That's an excellent idea. Shall we meet in the morning before breakfast and take a ride?" asked Jane, unable to keep the enthusiasm from her voice.

"At seven, then."

Jane presented herself at the stables at the appointed hour. Her pleasure at the idea of a bracing gallop soon waned when she saw the mount that Henry led out for her.

"Are you sure you can't manage something with a little more . . . spirit?" she asked.

"I don't want it on my head if you fall and hurt yourself," replied Henry as he regarded the lumbering old mare he had led out. "Bessie ain't so bad. Nice gait."

"I'm sure," she remarked dryly. "Nonetheless, I assure you it would be best to try another animal." She eyed the horse he had led out for himself, a full-chested bay stallion standing nearly sixteen hands. "This one would do nicely."

"But, miss," sputtered the head groom, "that's a blooded stallion . . ."

"Would you kindly put the sidesaddle on him." Jane smiled sweetly but unconsciously a tone of command had crept into her voice.

Henry opened his mouth to argue, but stopped. "Very well," he muttered, motioning to a young groom. "It's your own funeral, though Mrs. Fairchild will have my hide if she has to hire a new governess."

When the boy returned with the stallion and a new mount for the head groom, Henry lifted her into the saddle, then swung himself up.

"Lead the way, miss. Let us see what you can do."

An hour later the two of them walked their tired horses back into the courtyard.

"What fun," exclaimed Jane as she was helped down. "I have so missed riding."

"Fun!" remarked Henry as he wiped his brow. "Lord Almighty, miss. Where did you ever learn to ride like that?"

Jane laughed. "Do I pass your test?"

The groom bowed and tipped his cap to her. "Miss, the stables are at your command."

Things had gone very well, she mused as she walked along the path that led over the sloping pastureland toward the neighboring village. Henry had chosen a docile, well-mannered pony for Peter's first lesson. Though nearly stiff with fright, the boy had allowed her to lift him into the saddle, where his knuckles turned white from clenching the reins. But after the second circle around the paddock, her at the horse's head leading it in a slow walk, he had visibly relaxed, the drawn look around his mouth loosening into a tentative smile. Twenty minutes was all Jane allowed, not wanting to push him too much. Afterward she was gratified to hear him tell Henry, as he helped put the tack away, that they would be back at the same time tomorrow.

She smiled to herself, remembering his look of wonderment when he discovered he could do it. Had Nanna felt such delight in teaching her? The thought made her pat her pocket guiltily, the letter from Mrs. Fairchild to her old nurse safely ensconced within the capacious folds of material. She had seen the letter lying on the sideboard and had offered to take it to the village. Truly she had looked forward to a brisk walk and some time to herself—and truly she disliked subterfuge—but in this case it was imperative, she reminded herself. Still, she disliked misleading Mrs. Fairchild, for here she was, on her way home and the letter was still in her pocket. In order to distract her nagging conscience, she began to pay particular attention to her surroundings.

Stately copses of elm and oak separated vast rolling pasturelands and fields of wheat in this section of the estate. The tenant cottages that she passed seemed snug and well cared-for—there was just one that seemed to be missing a section of thatch on its roof. She must speak to the steward about it.

That brought another smile to her face. She had first met the man three weeks ago and had immediately pointed out some minor repair that he should attend to at the stables. The man had gaped at her as if she had had maggots in her head. "What did you say?" he had asked incredulously. She had calmly repeated her request, her gaze unwavering until he had stammered that he would look into it. Poor Mr. Fielding, it must have nearly given him a fit of vapors. But the repair had been made.

The next day she had cornered him again with another small problem. Now, he was almost used to it. In fact he was even essaying a feeble smile whenever she approached and would pull out his notebook in readiness for her. She would have to remember to tell him to look at the cottage's roof. At least the marquess, despite his other faults, was not a tightfisted landlord.

Jane lifted her face to the warmth of the late afternoon sun. Blackbirds chirped from atop the tall hawthorne hedge that bordered the footpath and as she came to an opening in the stile she saw a profusion of wildflowers among the tall grasses. Impulsively, she turned into the field and gathered a large bouquet, pressing the fragrant blossoms up close to her face and breathing deeply. She twirled around like a little girl, all at once overcome with a giddy feeling of freedom. What a crazy thought, she chided herself. She was but a servant! Yet she had so many fewer constrictions and rules than before—and she wasn't bored. For the first time in her life she felt she was doing something meaningful.

Impishly lifting the hem of her skirts, she gave rein to her high spirits and began to run back toward the path. She raced through the stile, then suddenly was engulfed by a dark shadow. A muffled oath followed, then the sound of thundering hooves brought up short. She skittered to a halt and looked at a very large black stallion which was tossing its head and dancing nervously only a few yards from where she stood.

"Damnation! Have you no more sense, girl, than to run out in front of a galloping horse?" The rider eyed Jane's shabby gray gown and bonnet, the tendrils of mousy hair escaping from under its unflattering brim, and made a grimace of distaste.

Jane looked up at him. Above a pair of gleaming Hessians, impeccable buckskins encased well-muscled thighs that were having no trouble controlling his skittish mount. Despite the sudden stop the perfectly tailored riding coat showed not a crease around the broad shoulders, nor was the knotted cravat even slightly askew. Jane shifted her glance upward. The man's features were perfectly chiseled, handsome but hard, with a cold, haughty look to them. His locks, where they tumbled out from under his curly-brimmed beaver hat, were as dark as his stallion's coat. And the eyes, a sea green color, were flooded with annoyance.

Piqued at being spoken to—and looked at—like that, Jane replied without thinking.

"And you have no sense, sir, than to gallop recklessly along a footpath?" Some impulse made her add, "Or perhaps you cannot control your mount."

The eyes now betrayed a flash of anger. "If I could not control my mount you would be very lucky to be alive," he retorted. Then, as if realizing the ignominity of brangling with a farm girl, his face composed itself back to its frozen haughtiness. This infuriated Jane even more.

Heedless of the propriety, she addressed another bold sally at him.

"This would never have happened if you had not been trespassing. I'll have you know these are the Marquess of Saybrook's lands."

"Ah. Saybrook." The corners of his mouth twitched imperceptibly. "Then aren't you trespassing as well? And stealing, perhaps?" He looked pointedly at her chest.

Jane was momentarily nonplussed. She looked guiltily at the flowers still clutched to her bosom. "I'm not . . . er, that is . . . Of course I'm not stealing!" she replied indignantly. "I'm taking these to the manor house. I work there."

A look of surprise creased the rider's brow. "Indeed? And just how, pray, are you employed there?"

Jane lifted her chin. The nerve of the man, to question her word! "I am the new governess."

"The governess," he repeated, staring intently at her.

Jane's anger, sparked more than she cared to admit by the shock of the near accident, had just as quickly died down. And now, under the penetrating gaze of the gentleman on horseback, she realized just what a predicament her hasty words had put her in. Not only had she nearly caused him to unseat himself and possibly injure a valuable horse, but she—a servant—had been unspeakably rude to him. It was entirely possible that he was an acquaintance of the marquess's, and one word about today's incident would no doubt result in her instant dismissal. What a mull she had made of her first encounter with the gentry!

"Oh dear." The words escaped without her even realizing it.

The gentleman had been watching the turmoil on her face. "What's the matter?" he inquired. "Did Hero hurt you after all?"

"N . . . n . . . n . . . no," she stammered. "It's not that." She stopped for a second, then decided she had no alternative but to throw herself at his mercy, much as the idea stuck in her throat. "It's just that this is my first position and . . . and I have not yet . . . I fear I wasn't thinking—I was terribly rude, sir. I beg your pardon." Her eyes didn't dare meet his for fear he would see not contrition but indignation at having to humble herself to such a haughty gentleman.

"Having such a fright would cause anyone to forget her manners," he allowed.

The quick flare of anger in her face nearly made him laugh aloud. So the effort at being apologetic was costing her dearly!

But just as quickly, Jane managed a semblance of a smile. "Thank you for your generosity, sir," she said through gritted teeth. There was another pause. "I would ask for your further generosity in not mentioning this incident to Lord Saybrook."

He paused as if to consider the request. "Let us agree that what has happened will remain between you and me alone," he replied with a sardonic smile. "However . . ."

Jane took a deep breath, waiting to hear the rest.

" . . . it is to be hoped that the governess can learn her lessons well, too." With that he put the spurs to his impatient stallion and set off at an easy canter.

"Wretch," she muttered at the broad back fast disappearing down the path. "Arrogant, high in the instep, conceited . . ." She kicked at a stone in her frustration. "Insufferable." He had certainly gotten the better of her. All the way home she consoled her wounded pride by repeating every disparaging adjective that she had learned from Thomas to describe the odious gentleman. At least, she consoled herself, it was most unlikely she would ever have to see him again.

She felt tolerably composed by the time she walked into the manor through the kitchen door, even though the mere thought of those sea green eyes still set her teeth on edge. Usually the warmth and the heady smells emanating from Cook's domain were ever so soothing. Perhaps she would linger over a glass of warm milk and fresh scones. Then her spirits would be truly restored.

Instead of the normal calm however, Jane had walked into a scene straight out of Bedlam. Upstairs maids were scurrying with piles of linen, Cook was standing, arms akimbo, shouting orders at spooked scullery maids, and poor Mrs. Fairchild was wringing her hands, muttering, "Oh dear, oh dear," to no one in particular.

"What on earth is the matter?" cried Jane.

Mrs. Fairchild looked up at her. "Oh there you are. Thank goodness you have returned. He wants to see you."

"*Who* does?"

"Why, the master, of course. He has arrived! Unannounced! His rooms must be put in order. Cook is worried about turning out a decent supper in this space of time and I . . . the house!" She moaned faintly.

"Now, Mrs. Fairchild, don't be a goose. The house is faultless, as you well know—why, the floors and furniture fairly glisten with beeswax and there isn't a speck of dust anywhere."

The older woman managed a wan smile. "I suppose things aren't *too* shabby, but I should hate to disappoint his lordship. Oh, he asked that you present yourself to him in the library at six."

"Very well. Now calm yourself."

Mrs. Fairchild nodded. "Yes, of course." She cleared her throat, then added, "You will be punctual? Mr. Edward does not tolerate sloppy habits at Highwood."

Jane nodded, not trusting her tone of voice to hide her true feelings. From what she knew so far of the man, she didn't give a fig for what the Marquess of Saybrook could tolerate—she certainly found it hard to tolerate the apprehension he seemed to bring out in everyone at Highwood.

Even the footmen and parlor maids were affected by the air of nervousness that had descended upon the house. They rushed about, unloading the traveling carriage and freshening the rooms with a hushed seriousness, engaging in none of the usual cheerful banter. Jane did not even receive so much as a smile from any of the distracted servants as she made her way up to her room to make ready for her first interview with her employer. Heaven knows she needed to freshen up her hair and gown—she must look a fright after all that had happened.

The mirror over the washstand told her that she wasn't wrong. A goodly number of tendrils had worked their way loose from the severe bun at the nape of her neck and dangled in disarray around her ears and throat. Behind the errant curls there was a distinct smudge on her left cheek. The wildflowers, still clutched in her hands, had scattered their petals across the bodice of her gown while its hem was covered with dust. It was hardly a picture to inspire confidence in an employer. She sighed longingly as she thought of her abigail and a nice hot bath. Then she began to scrub the dirt from her face and to rearrange her hair.

Jane found that she was curious to finally meet the marquess. She knew his house, his lands, his possessions, his dependents, and his servants. From that she had formed a very definite picture of him. And now she was to meet him in person.

She finished sponging the hem of her gown, for she had decided not to change into her better gray merino one but to remain in the distinctly less flattering shade of brown. As she regarded her reflection she almost grimaced at the plain, rather unattractive face that peered back at her. But, she sighed, it had been decided that it was best to look as unremarkable as possible—not that it seemed to matter here at Highwood. Well, the hairstyle certainly accomplished that, along with the walnut leaf rinse which had dulled her once glorious hair to an insipid shade nearly as ugly as that of the dress.

She picked up a pair of spectacles from the dresser. Though only made of clear glass, they added an even dowdier touch to her appearance. She had made sure to wear them occasionally around the house, so everyone was used to seeing them on her. Propping them firmly on the bridge of her nose, she felt ready to meet his lordship. Now, if she could just remember to squint. . . . A knock on the door interrupted her thoughts. Mrs. Fairchild had left nothing to chance. She dutifully followed Glavin downstairs to the library.

He was standing with his back to her, seemingly engrossed in the blazing hearth when Jane quietly entered the room. She stopped near the threshold, not merely out of deference but out of surprise. The gentleman before her was over six feet tall, with long legs, narrow hips, and a broad, muscular back, accentuated by the snug cut of his elegant swallow-tailed coat of claret superfine. There was a lazy, catlike grace that radiated from his person, as well as something that hinted at a veiled power beneath the lean, hard body. Thick, dark hair— *not* gray, very dark—fell to the back of his collar while his shirt points were moderate, allowing him to turn his head with ease. Her surprise turned to shock when he did so. Those sea green eyes!

"You!" she blurted out.

"Please take a seat—Miss Langley, is it?" he said coolly, neither his voice nor expression giving the slightest acknowledgement that they had ever laid eyes on each other before. He motioned to a wing chair while he seated himself at a massive oak desk facing her.

Jane sat, too stunned to say anything.

Lord Saybrook let the silence last what seemed to be an interminable amount of time before continuing.

"I must congratulate you on your progress with my ward during the short time you have been here. He seems to have actually learned something."

She had recovered her wits enough to detect the faint note of sarcasm in his voice. "I take it you have no high opinion of governesses then, my lord?"

"No," he admitted. "I do not. Most of them I have met have been either vapid or cruel. But you appear to be neither."

Jane kept her eyes focused on her primly folded hands resting in her lap. How was one to respond to such a compliment, if compliment it was?

"I wonder that you would bother hiring one at all," she said softly.

"It is necessary," was the curt reply. There was another silence. "I have also found my ward to be more . . . lively. I take it I have you to thank for this as well?"

Jane couldn't resist the opening. "Oh, it is really nothing, my lord. Children naturally respond to a little love and attention." She smiled innocently. "His name is Peter, by the way—in case you have forgotten."

A flush stole across his face, she noted with satisfaction, and his jaw set grimly. So, she had managed to effect a crack in his icy manner. But when he spoke, his voice was quite even.

"You may go now."

Without any further ado, he turned his attention to the papers on his desk.

It was Jane's turn to feel the heat of anger. To be dismissed like a . . . a servant! But as soon as she thought it, the very irony of the situation nearly made her smile in spite of herself. She rose silently and left the room, conceding the last word to him. After all, he had had an unfair advantage in the meeting. But she felt she had held her own, and had even scored a hit herself.

Yet the whole meeting had infuriated her, only serving to confirm her suspicion that the marquess was a cold, hard man. When she reached her own chamber she was still fuming over the bored, sardonic look on his face, the way his eyes raked over her as if they didn't even see her. She made a vow that he would never intimidate her as he seemed to have done the rest of the household. Not that it mattered. From what she understood, his lordship never stayed more than a week or two at a time. But if he wanted to cross wills with her, she was ready!

The thick oriental carpet muffled the sound of Saybrook's well-polished Hessians as he paced before the fire in his library. The polished paneling glowed in the flickering light, conjuring up evenings long past when he would creep in to find his mother reading by the fire. The memories caused a sudden lurch in his chest, a longing to make this his home again, a place of warmth, of laughter, of life rather than a place he avoided as much as possible. He loved the smell of the leather books, the familiar furniture, the carved moldings—missing one acorn that he had whittled away with a new pocket knife.

. . . He shook his head as if to banish the painful thoughts.

They plagued him whenever he came back. Most of the time he was able to keep them at bay. So good had he become at hiding his feelings he could almost believe he had none, none at all. Perhaps that was why he felt half dead.

His lips compressed. Thank God it was only a couple of weeks a year that he had to return to deal with his affairs. His steward was a capable, honest man who ran the lands well. There was no doubt that all would be in order and decisions could be made swiftly. Of course, he would inspect things himself and see that his tenants had been looked after properly. But that shouldn't take too long.

And Mrs. Fairchild ran the manor as well as his mother had. A poor relation from that side of the family, Mrs. Fairchild had come to Highwood when he was still in leading strings. Saybrook grimaced as he remembered how many times she had borne the brunt of some childish prank of his or Liza's—it was a wonder she did not hold him in the greatest distaste! But her good nature never wavered and now she was delighted with the responsibility of caring for his estate and ward while he absented himself for months on end. . . . Did she have an inkling as to his reasons? He sometimes thought she looked at him with—no matter. She ran the house and servants with a gentle, yet firm hand.

Saybrook allowed himself a small smile. Servants. Most of them had been there for years. The governess was the only new face—and a rather interesting, if dowdy one at that. He almost chuckled, recalling her look of dismay at discovering her errant rider and new employer were one in the same. Oh, she had tried to hide her emotions, but her expressive features did not cooperate. Miss Langley would make a poor gambler, for what she was thinking was quite clear. He thought back to the afternoon. She had been quite angry at his manner. It made him curious as to how a girl of her position would challenge her betters, but he shrugged it off. No matter that her manner was sadly deficient for a servant, he rather liked a show of spirit. Manners she would soon learn.

More importantly, she had done wonders with his ward. The boy was less painfully shy, though there was still a wariness in his eyes that shouldn't be there in one so young. Saybrook ran his hands through his thick locks. It was his own fault, he knew, if the boy was afraid of him. He should spend more time with him, but . . .

He kept pacing, lost in thought, until Glavin knocked to inform him that his supper was served. With a heavy sigh he left the library, wishing that the short stay was already at an end.

Jane took supper in the kitchen with Mrs. Fairchild and Peter, as had become their habit. It was informal and cozy, with the delicious smells emanating from the copper pots and Cook's constant stream of banter and neighborhood gossip. She felt the atmosphere was good for the boy, and no one argued with her—indeed no one argued with any suggestion she made around Highwood, but seemed to accept her suggestions naturally.

Mrs. Fairchild was still distracted and monitored every dish that was carried to the dining room, much to Cook's offense. So Jane forbore questioning her about his lordship, though there were many things she wished to know about. She was not so reticent when she took Peter up to bed.

"I thought you told me your uncle was old?" she said as they climbed the stairs.

Peter looked perplexed. "Why, he is, Miss Jane. I heard Mrs. Fairchild say he is nearly eight-and-twenty."

"Oh, ancient!" Jane laughed and rolled her eyes. How silly of her.

After she had finished reading to Peter she noticed that he seemed restless and loath to see her go. So after putting the book aside she sat on the edge of the bed and fondly brushed the locks from his forehead.

"Are you happy your uncle has come for a visit?"

Peter gave her a strange look then cast his eyes down to his blanket.

"He doesn't like me," he finally blurted out.

Jane's arm slipped around his frail shoulders and squeezed gently. "Why, Peter, what fustian! Of course he likes you," she said with forced cheerfulness while fearing that with a child's natural perception he had indeed sensed the truth. "You must realize that your uncle is very busy, with many demands on his time. I'm sure he does not mean you to think he doesn't care," she added lamely.

The boy nodded miserably. She could feel his shoulder hunch under her touch and found herself wondering whether the poignant scene would wipe the arrogant sneer from Lord Saybrook's face. Remembering the cold, carefully controlled manner of earlier in the evening, she doubted it. And it made her dislike his lordship even more. But she couldn't bear to see Peter so downcast. Without thinking, she came up with a plan.

"How would you like to surprise your uncle—and make him very proud of you?"

The boy looked up in wonder. "How?"

"I heard Henry talking about the village fair. There is to be a riding competition, one for children as well as adults. I think you've come along so nicely you should be part of it. We'll make it a surprise."

"I don't know," he faltered. "I don't . . . do you really think . . ."

She squeezed him harder. "Of course you can! You and Tarquin are best of friends now and you've been off the lead for days. By week's end you'll· be trotting and shall be quite ready for the fair."

"He might not be there." Peter was trying to keep the growing excitement out of his voice.

"Oh, he'll be there. Leave that to me." Jane smiled grimly. As she well knew, any of the surrounding gentry in residence would be bound by tradition to put in an appearance. And furthermore, if she had to jam a pistol into his elegant ribs, Lord Saybrook would be there. Of course it was to be hoped that such extreme measures would not be necessary. Surely even an unfeeling guardian could not begrudge such a small demand on his time. But she would deal with that later. Right now she was rewarded by seeing the look of happiness on the boy's face.

"It will be a *big* surprise, will it not?" he said with unconcealed delight.

"Indeed it will. We'll practice extra hard this week— but mind you, you mustn't neglect your lessons. And now, you had better get some sleep. We have a lot of work to do."

She planted a kiss on the top of his head and tucked him under the covers.

"Good night, Miss Jane," murmured the boy as she walked toward the door with her candle. "And thank you."

She closed the door knowing full well she left a sleepy boy to dream happily of saddles and ponies and guardian uncles.

Chapter Four

Jane saw very little of Lord Saybrook over the next few days. He rose quite early each morning to ride out with his steward before she came down for breakfast. A few times she caught a glimpse of him striding into the house, where he disappeared into the library. In the evenings, he dined alone and then retreated to the sanctuary of the library again. The footmen mentioned that he retired quite late, sometimes past midnight.

So she had not had the chance to speak to him about the fair. He had certainly made no effort to have any further dealing with her—in fact, it was as if she didn't exist, she fumed, though why that irritated her she had no idea. Of course the lord of the manor would not concern himself about the governess.

He didn't concern himself about Peter either, she noted. The boy saw no more of him than she did, though more than once she had caught him staring wistfully out the window as his uncle rode off on Hero. Even she could not deny he was an excellent rider and cut a dashing figure on the spirited black stallion.

Jane was afraid she would have to take the drastic measure of requesting an audience with Lord Saybrook when she learned from Mrs. Fairchild that he would indeed be attending the fair.

"Oh yes, he'll be there," said the older woman one night after dinner in response to Jane's question. "Old Squire Hawkins stopped by yesterday to remind Mr. Edward. Oh, he tried to make an excuse, but the squire would hear none of it. He was a friend of Mr. Edward's father and has known his lordship since he was in short coats. He reminded him of his duty—he must be there for the blessing of the wheat."

Jane smiled to herself. The children's riding came right after that. It was perfect. She had merely to inform him before the ceremony that he should take a few minutes to watch his nephew.

The day of the fair dawned bright and clear. Jane smiled as Peter tried to contain his excitement. High boots, proper breeches, and a velvet-collared riding jacket had been unearthed from one of the myriad trunks in the attics. With his carefully combed hair and neat cap the boy was the picture of a little gentleman. Mrs. Fairchild and Cook, as well as Henry, had been let in on the plan and were as excited as Peter. They fussed over him throughout the meal, assuring him that he would acquit himself splendidly.

They were all careful to remain in the kitchen to avoid the off chance of running into his lordship and giving away the surprise. It seemed like ages, thought Jane as she smoothed the skirt of her gown—oh, what she wouldn't give for a proper riding habit—before Henry knocked at the scullery door to tell them that the master had ridden off and the coast was clear. It had been arranged that he would accompany them to the fair so that she would be free to seek out Lord Saybrook. Their horses were already saddled, and Jane was relieved to see that Peter's pony, Tarquin, was as placid as ever, having sensed none of the nervous excitement in the air that was making the other mounts tug restlessly at the reins held by one of the grooms.

She was also happy to see that Peter showed no hesitation or last-minute nerves as Henry lifted him into the saddle. There was only a look of anticipation on his face. Jane, too, felt caught up in the same mood. Lost in her own reveries, she barely took notice of the spirited banter between Henry and Peter. It was only with a start that she realized they had arrived at the fair. They halted near a large paddock where the riding competition would be held. She guided her horse next to Peter's and, leaning over, she put her hand over one of his small ones. She looked into his eyes and smiled, then gave him a squeeze. He smiled back.

She dismounted, leaving her horse and Peter in Henry's care, and walked toward the crowd of people milling around the rough stage erected for the fair. It should be no trouble to find Lord Saybrook—she had already seen the big black stallion tethered away from the other horses.

Indeed it was no trouble at all. A quick glance showed the top of his brushed beaver hat towering above the group of local squires with whom he was engaged. She noted the lazy way he leaned against the stage, his carved whip tapping his polished boot as if to punctuate his boredom as he listened to the conversation. Now and then he would smile faintly and reply to some comment, but for the most part he stood silent, aloof.

A rustling at the podium indicated that the local parson was preparing to deliver his little speech, so the group of gentry began to drift away from the stage to take up position with the rest of the crowd. Jane took the opportunity to approach Lord Saybrook.

"Excuse me, my lord." She stepped directly in his path so he was obliged to stop.

"Ah, Miss . . . Langley." It was said as if he were struggling to remember just who she was. He gave her a pointed look, taking in her dowdy gown, unflattering bonnet, and most particularly the spectacles perched on her nose. "Pray, what is it?"

Despite herself, Jane felt a flush of embarrassment steal over her in response to his scrutiny. It quickly turned to anger—damn the man, she fumed. How did he always manage to irritate her so quickly? But remembering her purpose, she reined in her temper and spoke.

"It is your ward, Peter, sir. He is to ride in the children's competition . . ."

Saybrook's eyebrow shot up. "You must be joking, Miss Langley. Peter is terrified of horses."

"*Was*," corrected Jane, a little more sharply than she intended. "Peter *was* terrified of horses, as was only natural. But he has overcome his fear. It would be . . . very much appreciated if you would be present to watch him."

A portly gentleman with wispy gray hair and a reddened face that bespoke of too much claret was gesturing at Saybrook with the tip of his gold-chased cane. Beside him, two ladies looking dreadfully out of place in the latest London fashions added their smiles to the gentleman's entreaties.

Saybrook nodded his greetings. "Thank you, Miss Langley. Now, if you will excuse me." He turned and walked to meet the other group.

Jane could barely restrain herself from directing a kick at his well-tailored behind. Dismissed again in such an insolent manner! Well, at least she had accomplished her task. It was really of no consequence how he treated her as long as Peter was happy.

The parson had begun to speak and she remained where she was, casting a sideways look every so often at

Saybrook and his friends. After exchanging pleasantries, he had gracefully stepped into the proffered space between the two ladies. On second glance one of them appeared much older than the other. Mother and daughter, she guessed. Or mother, daughter, and father she added to herself. No doubt they were angling after the marquess, judging from the effusive smiles and simpering manner of the ladies. With his title and lands he would be quite a catch on the Marriage Mart. The fact that he had been abroad for so long accounted for the fact that she had not known who he was.

Her thoughts were interrupted by the crowd beginning to move off as the parson finished his speech. The smell of savory pies filled the air, as did the lilting notes of the fiddlers. Farmers drifted to the exhibition of livestock while their wives and children clustered around displays of ribbons and candy. Jane stayed where she was. She had always enjoyed the sights and sounds of a country fair and was now taking a moment to drink it all in. And of course she had to admit that she wanted the satisfaction of seeing the haughty marquess accede to her request.

To her shock, however, she saw him move off with the gentleman and two ladies, not in the direction of the riding but toward an area where long trestle tables had been set up next to a group of laughing farmhands dispensing ale and mulled cider. She remained rooted to the ground for a moment, unable to believe that anyone could be so selfish and cruel. In her mind's eye, she could picture the look of dejection on Peter's face, the slump of the frail shoulders so used to disappointment. It goaded her into action.

With nary a regard for the propriety of her actions she hurried after his lordship's party. Coming up close behind them, she called out firmly, "Lord Saybrook, may I have a word with you—in private."

All four people turned around, different degrees of surprise registering on their faces. The gentleman frowned at Jane's temerity while his wife exclaimed, "Well, I never . . . Who *is* this woman?"

Saybrook had a faintly sardonic smile on his face as he seemed to ponder just how great a scene Jane would cause if he refused her request. "My ward's governess."

"Such manners! Turn her out instantly," said the woman as if Jane weren't there. "I shall be more than happy to give you my recommendations . . ."

Saybrook interrupted her. "I trust you will excuse me for a moment."

The woman sniffed in the air and turned on her heel, taking her husband by the arm. As the younger woman turned as well, Jane realized with a start that she knew her. Miss Matilda Farrington. A flighty, insipid girl now entering her second Season. Jane had seen her at various routs and balls, and of course Almack's, and had disliked her instantly. The girl was one of those creatures who flirted shamelessly with any gentleman with a title, young or old. There was no need to fear recognition, however. The Miss Farrington didn't even deign to look at her as she lifted her elegant skirts and swooshed after her parents.

Saybrook followed Jane a little ways off, out of hearing of anyone around them. Still white hot with pent-up anger, Jane launched into a tirade with not a thought as to what she was saying.

"It is beyond belief," she said with a hiss, "that one man can be so selfish, so unfeeling, so . . . monstrous! Whether you choose to treat your acquaintances and your servants with disdain—oh, I see the haughty sneer on your face—is entirely your own concern. But that

you would deliberately hurt a child is outside of enough!
Are you too blind to see that Peter is craving for your
notice, for your approval, though Lord knows why. If
you don't take a few minutes of your precious time to do
your duty as a guardian . . ." She was so beside herself
that she didn't know quite how to finish the sentence.
"Oooh," she sputtered, "if I were a man, I'd horsewhip
you!"

Saybrook had gone rigid and his face was absolutely
drained of color.

"And you needn't bother telling me I'm turned out!"
she added. "I will pack immediately."

Turning on her heel, she stalked off, not bothering to
note the marquess's reaction. Now that she had vented
her anger she felt drained, almost too weak to walk. But
she took a deep breath and kept her chin up, refusing to
let him see her waver.

She made her way to where Henry had tethered the
horses. Had she really said such things to the marquess?
She was lucky he hadn't called the constables to haul her
off to Bedlam. With a sigh, she had to admit that her
brother was right—there were times when she could be
quite . . . rash.

Before mounting, she looked to where the riding competition was taking place. Peter was in the middle of the
ring, trotting in a neat circle. She felt a rush of pride at
how straight he sat in the saddle and how well he guided
his pony. From the corner of her eye she saw Saybrook
leaning stiffly against the fence, watching as well. So, at
least she had accomplished something other than getting
turned out without references! Peter would be in raptures, no matter that it was a false happiness.

The judges suddenly motioned Peter toward a little
jump standing at one end of the ring. Jane bit her lip in
alarm. Peter had never attempted such a thing, but he

was cantering toward it with nary a hesitation. Up went Tarquin, and for a moment it seemed that the boy would be left behind. But he regained his balance and kept his seat. The small crowd burst into applause. So did Saybrook. Peter reined in close to his guardian, a shy smile on his face. To her great surprise, the marquess vaulted over the fence and patted Peter on his thigh. Even from where she was she could see the happiness on the boy's face. Well, she thought, at least the marquess could do his duty handsomely if he tried.

Peter was awarded a blue ribbon, then walked his horse, with Saybrook still at its head, toward where the marquess's own stallion was tethered. Jane sighed and mounted her own horse. She had enjoyed it at Highwood. Now what was she to do? On the ride back, she rued her blasted quick tongue. Once again, it had landed her in the suds.

Jane sat on her bed surveying the meager pile of belongings ready to be packed in her small trunk. She suddenly realized that she had not enough money for the coach ride back to her father's estate, even if she took outside passage. Certainly, there was nothing for an inn. To be sure she was owed some amount for the time she had spent at Highwood, but she could not bring herself to ask Lord Saybrook for anything. With a slight frown of dismay she wondered whether she might have to sleep in a field tonight. And she hadn't even decided if she would go home in any case—but what was she to do?

In the middle of mulling over the problem, a knock came at the door. She sighed and bid whomever it was to enter. Perhaps Mrs. Fairchild had heard of her firing and had come to say good-bye. If so, Jane decided that she might be able to bring herself to borrow a few shillings from her. But most likely it was a footman, ready to toss her out the door, she thought glumly. Which was no doubt what she deserved.

The door opened slowly and Peter's smiling face appeared behind it. He rushed to her arms, already talking excitedly.

"Did you see my ribbon?" he demanded, not waiting for an answer. "I was a little scared—but just a little—but I knew I could do it! Uncle Edward says that it was a tip-top performance!"

"It was indeed."

"And I'm to have supper with him in the real dining room. With silver candlesticks and champagne!"

Jane laughed. "Oh very grand."

"Yes," continued the boy, "and I asked if you could come too . . ."

"Peter!" she exclaimed. "You . . ."

" . . . and he said yes of course, and that I should come and ask you to join us."

Jane was thrown into a state of confusion. "But, Peter," she said gently, "it's not proper for a servant to dine with the master."

He looked at her in consternation. "But why not? Uncle Edward said it was quite all right."

"He didn't say exactly that, I'll wager," she muttered, but she didn't have the heart to spoil the boy's day. If the marquess could bear it, so could she. "All right then, I shall be delighted to attend."

"He says to be there at seven."

"I shall come by your room at quarter of. You must look your best if you are to grace his lordship's table."

When the boy had hurried off, she sank down on her bed, relieved that at least for tonight she didn't have to worry about where she would sleep. Surely he wouldn't expect her to leave in the dead of night? As she considered the matter she thought some more about Lord Saybrook himself. He must have a softer side, one she certainly hadn't seen yet, not to want to spoil Peter's enjoyment of the day. After all, it was going well beyond the bounds of duty to include her at his dining table, especially after what had taken place. Why, the very sight of her must put him off his appetite! And obviously Peter had not been told she was leaving. She shook her head. It had been a very strange day.

At the stroke of seven Jane ushered Peter into the dining room. It was a vast space, with dark oak paneling and an impressive chandelier that winked sparkles of light from the myriad candles in among the crystal. The table was just as imposing, massive with carved legs and a breadth that seemed to dwarf the three place settings at the end nearest the stone fireplace.

Lord Saybrook was already in the room. A glass of champagne in his hand, he stood by the crackling blaze, staring into the flames as if lost in thought. She noticed with a start how very handsome he was, now that his face didn't have the cold, sardonic look that normally played on his features. Silhouetted by the firelight, his profile seemed softer, more vulnerable. At the sound of their steps he looked up, and the moment was gone. His mouth hardened and his eyes became cooler.

Thought she had donned her best black merino gown, Jane felt a flush of self-consciousness as she observed Saybrook regarding her. His superbly tailored black coat fit him to perfection, understated, yet elegant, and a waistcoat of burgundy silk showed beneath it. A white linen shirt rose to moderate points and the starched neckcloth fell in a perfect waterfall. His riding breeches had been replaced by pantaloons which fit snugly over a pair of soft Moroccan boots—he had certainly "dressed" for dinner. Jane felt woefully dowdy, then realized it was most likely exactly how she was supposed to feel.

With exaggerated politeness, Saybrook bowed slightly to her and indicated the chair to his right.

"Peter, perhaps you will do the honors with Miss Langley's chair."

Jane had not dared meet his gaze as yet, not knowing quite what to expect, or how to react. When she finally did so, his eyes betrayed no emotion at all, as if nothing untoward had occurred between them. For some reason, that made her feel even more uncomfortable.

Saybrook lifted the bottle of champagne from the silver cooler and filled the goblet at her place, then splashed a touch in Peter's glass.

"A toast. To Peter's equestrian accomplishments. My congratulations, lad."

The boy colored with pleasure as the two adults lifted their glasses. He sniffed at the bubbly drink then cautiously tasted it.

"It tickles!" he cried. "And it tastes awful."

"It improves with age—one's own, that is," remarked Saybrook dryly. "Don't you agree?"

Jane managed a nod.

Two footmen brought in the first course, and if they were surprised at seeing the boy and his governess dining with the master their impassive faces gave no hint of it, though Jane was sure it would be the talk of the servant's quarters.

Try as she might, Jane found it difficult to relax and take some enjoyment from the evening. Usually she would appreciate the irony inherent in the whole situation and would laugh at it, but tonight she felt only a certain glumness. Her reticence led to rather long lapses in the conversation, though she did notice that Saybrook made an effort to converse with Peter, something he obviously had little practice in doing. But the boy, still

flushed with excitement, was happy to prattle on, regardless.

Suddenly, the marquess spoke directly to her. "Do you
always wear spectacles?"

"Why, n . . . n . . . no," she faltered. "That is, they're
rather new and I don't need them all the time."

"Perhaps they are not suited to you."

"Why is that?" She was curious as to why he would
remark on it.

"Because you appear to be squinting most of the time.
Maybe you would be more comfortable if you removed
them."

Flustered, Jane plucked them off her nose and shoved
them into her pocket.

"An improvement," murmured Saybrook, a slight
twitch at the corners of his mouth.

"How would you know that?" she demanded.

"To your appearance," he shot back.

Jane lowered her eyes to her plate. So that was his
plan in inviting her to dine—to humiliate her in payment
for what she had done that afternoon before he turned
her out. She bit off any retort, determined not to give
him the satisfaction of knowing he had discomforted her.

When the final covers had been removed, Saybrook
turned to Peter. "And what do you usually do until your
bedtime?"

"Miss Langley has been teaching me to play chess."

His eyebrows shot up. "Chess? How interesting. Why
don't you run along and set up the board in the drawing
room while Miss Langley and I have a word together in
the library."

Jane rose wordlessly. No doubt he had been savoring
this moment throughout dinner. But she smiled to herself. There was really nothing else he could do to her—
she was already fired.

She followed him into the library, where a fire blazed, casting a rosy glow to the polished wood paneling. Saybrook walked deliberately to the side table and poured himself a brandy. He swirled it around in his glass, then went to stand by the fire. Jane, too, remained on her feet, though he had gestured for her to take a seat. The marquess leaned an elbow on the mantel and crossed his legs nonchalantly. But instead of speaking right away, he kept his gaze riveted on the glass in his hand.

Jane lifted her chin imperceptibly, thinking that he was probably enjoying himself. She was sure he was about to ring a blistering peal over her head, but on consideration, she had to admit that she deserved it. Her behavior had been outside the pale this afternoon. It was a wonder that Saybrook had allowed her to set foot back in his house, not to speak of actually sitting down to dine with her. It must have cost him a considerable effort, for which he was entitled to be repaid. She resolved to bear his tirade in silence, keep her tongue in check, and leave with as much of her dignity intact as she could.

When he finally raised his eyes, Jane was surprised to see not anger but a strange expression that she couldn't fathom. Disconcerted, she dropped her own eyes and waited for him to speak.

"You are packed?" he asked quietly.

She nodded.

There was a pause as if he expected her to say something. Perhaps he thought she would beg for another chance? She knew things were way too far gone for that and remained silent.

His fingers drummed on the polished wood. He took a sip of the liquor in his glass. Then abruptly, he spoke again.

"You should remain at Highwood—if you please." Though the last words were added grudgingly, it was more of a statement than a request.

"You must be joking," said Jane. It was the last thing she had expected. "After what happened this afternoon . . ."

Saybrook ignored her. "The change in Peter has been nothing short of remarkable. I prefer that he stay in your care. I will make it worth your while—consider your salary doubled."

She stared at him in disbelief. "You cannot buy people, my lord!"

He smiled, a cold, bitter smile. "I just have. You *are* staying, aren't you?"

"For Peter's sake, yes," she replied. "But I shall not accept a single penny more than what Mrs. Fairchild hired me for."

"Suit yourself."

All vows of curbing her tongue went flying out the window. "And if I didn't think that the poor child needed someone to show him a little warmth and affection, don't think for a moment that I would remain here another instant."

"Another reminder of how sadly my character is lacking. How kind of you to inform me," remarked Saybrook, his voice heavy with sarcasm. "Pray, may I request that the next time you feel obliged to inform me of my countless defects in character you choose to do it in a private manner such as this." He had not raised his tone, but his voice was taut with barely controlled anger.

Jane could think of nothing to say. Part of her was furious at his high-handed manner, while part of her acknowledged his right to be angered and humiliated by her actions at the fair. And part of her was happy that she didn't have to leave Highwood.

"Am I excused, my lord?"

"Indeed you are not," he muttered. "But yes, you may go."

She hurried through the door, letting it shut with something suspiciously like a slam.

Saybrook swore under his breath and downed the glass in a single swallow.

"You had best keep an eye on your king's knight," cautioned Jane.

Peter looked up at her quickly, an accusing look breaking his mask of concentration. "I was going to move it," he said. "To there." His small fingers grasped the ivory figure and placed it near her queen.

Jane frowned in mock consternation. "I seem to be in the suds now. Peter, you have gotten quite good at this."

The boy grinned as she pondered how to allow him to checkmate her without being too obvious. Suddenly she was aware of a shadow falling over her.

"Uncle Edward! I have Miss Jane in check," announced Peter.

Saybrook surveyed the board. He was still dressed formally in black but his cravat had been loosened, giving him a more informal look, and his hands were thrust into his trouser pockets.

"Indeed you have. And your response, Miss Langley?"

Jane moved her piece. It was a clever piece of thinking which gave the boy a victory only if he was advanced enough to see it.

Saybrook's face remained impassive at her move, but he watched Peter intently. The boy studied the board carefully, taking his time. When he made to advance his bishop, he hesitated, almost making the wrong move, then quickly corrected himself and placed it on a different square.

"Check!"

"Mate," added the marquess softly. "Well done, lad." He smiled faintly at the boy, who beamed with pleasure.

Jane tipped her queen over in defeat. "And now, young man, I think it's well past your bedtime."

For a moment, it looked as if Peter might try to argue, but then his face brightened. "Oh, very well. I want to hear what happens to Rowena."

Saybrook cocked an eyebrow at Jane. "Rowena?"

"It is *Ivanhoe,* my lord," she replied as she rose from her chair. "Sir Scott's novel. I trust you do not disapprove—it was in the schoolroom library."

"I am familiar with it," he remarked dryly. "Illiteracy is not one of my faults."

Jane flushed.

Turning back to the boy, he asked, "Does Miss Langley read to you every night?"

"Oh yes. It is very exciting. There was a joust and Ivanhoe was very brave, but he was hurt and . . . would you like to listen, too?"

Saybrook looked surprised.

"Peter," said Jane softly, "I'm sure his lordship has more important . . ."

"Yes, I would." To Jane's amazement, he reached out his hand to the boy and the two of them headed for the stairs together, leaving Jane to follow behind.

When Peter was settled into his bed, Jane placed the candle on the nightstand and moved her chair closer to the light. Opening the leatherbound volume to where they had left off, she began to read, furious with herself that her voice seemed a trifle unsteady. Saybrook had moved to take a chair, but leaned a shoulder against the wall, arms folded across his chest, near the foot of the bed. He had placed his own candle on the dresser, so his features were unreadable in the flickering shadows but his very presence was unsettling. She was sure he was intent on rattling her—why else had he sought their company when he had never done so before.

She read on, never raising her eyes from the pages, fighting to keep her voice even so that he wouldn't have the satisfaction of knowing he made her nervous.

The chapter seemed to go on forever. But thankfully she noted that the boy's eyes were beginning to droop and she closed the book.

"I think that's enough for today, Peter."

Peter voiced a sleepy protest, which was cut off in midsentence by a big yawn. She ruffled his hair. "It will wait till tomorrow."

"Okay." He sighed. "It's a ripping yarn, isn't it, Uncle Edward."

"Quite," came the reply from the shadows.

"Do you think I might ride with you sometime?" continued the boy. "Like tomorrow?"

"Peter," said Jane in a low voice, "you mustn't pester your uncle."

"I beg pardon . . ." apologized Peter, but Saybrook interrupted him.

"I must ride out with my steward in the morning but perhaps after lunch you would like to accompany me to see Fleming's sheep. I believe they are shearing tomorrow. That is, if Miss Langley agrees that it will not interfere with your lessons."

Jane could feel his eyes upon her.

"Oh, Miss Jane, may I?"

"If it pleases his lordship, of course you may. But only if you promise to go to sleep now. You've had quite enough excitement for one day." She couldn't refrain from smiling when she saw that the boy's eyes had closed before she had finished her sentence.

Once in the hallway Jane meant to hurry off to her room. For her, too, more than enough had happened to occupy her thoughts. But she was stopped by Saybrook's voice, low and quite close behind her.

"Do you play, Miss Langley?"

She turned in confusion. "Sir?"

"Chess," he replied. "It was a thoughtful move you made with Peter. I wondered if perhaps you have any skill whatsoever in the game. Or was it merely luck? Would you care to try—I find I don't feel quite ready to retire." His eyes locked with hers and the corners of his mouth quirked up in a faintly mocking smile. "But of course you may be tired after such a . . . trying day."

Jane could see the challenge in his gaze and sensed that he expected her to decline. So, though she had no desire to spend any more time in the marquess's company, she answered coolly, "I am not at all fatigued. If you command, I shall try to oblige you with an adequate match."

"It was not an order Miss Langley," he said softly. "It was a request."

"As I said, I am willing."

Saybrook led the way, to the library this time instead of the drawing room. He banked the fire into a roaring blaze and poured himself another brandy. On the corner of his desk was a magnificent ivory set arranged on a board of black-and-white marble. He motioned Jane to take a seat across from him and spun the board to offer her white.

She shook her head. "We shall draw for sides."

A slight smile creased his face. "As you wish."

Taking a pawn in each hand, he shuffled them behind his back and held out both fists toward her. She pointed to the right one. It opened to reveal a white one.

They played for over an hour in silence, each so intent on the play unfolding before them that their eyes never once met. Jane had been deliberating her next move for some minutes. She finally made up her mind and went to move her rook when suddenly the marquess's hand shot out, his long, slender fingers covering her own. She was so taken aback that she nearly knocked the remaining pieces from the board. He didn't release her, however, but said under his breath, "I should think you might want to think a moment more."

Flustered, her eyes roamed the board but all she was aware of was the feeling of strength he radiated, even though his touch was light, and how warm his fingers felt on hers. A faint flush stole to her cheeks and she bent her head lower, praying he wouldn't notice. Finally, his hand slipped from hers. He waited patiently, saying no more.

She gathered her wits enough to correct her mistake and was relieved that Saybrook continued on without another word. The end took no more than ten minutes. He executed a series of sophisticated attacks that left her defenseless.

"Oh, well played, my lord," she exclaimed in admiration. When she realized what she had said, another blush rose to her face. It was shocking to have spoken to him in such a friendly, familiar manner.

But instead of the set-down she expected, a genuine smile appeared fleetingly on Saybrook's face, the first she had ever seen.

"Approval from Miss Langley." He laughed. "Now that is high praise indeed!"

Jane averted her eyes. His tone had been light, bantering, but she chose to misunderstand it.

"I beg your pardon, my lord," she said stiffly. "I deserve your sarcasm for speaking to you in such a manner. I assure you I will endeavor to keep a rein on my tongue."

He shot her a penetrating look, as if trying to fathom her feelings. "It was not . . ." he began, then stopped abruptly. His face resumed its rigid lines. The moment was past.

"Where did you learn to play? You have some skill. It is not something I would expect from someone of your background."

Jane's spine stiffened. So he was back to insulting her. Odious man!

"No, of course you wouldn't. You have made it quite clear what you think of governesses." She noted he had the grace to color slightly at having his own bad manners flung back at him. "I became childhood friends with a squire's daughter, an only child, and was fortunate enough to be invited to share lessons with her. Her father taught us both to play, but only I had the inclination to continue. I daresay I learned a few things from him."

"I see. And what family was that?"

Jane had decided on the story of the squire's family to answer any questions about her background. It was safest to stay close to the truth, and the story was true for Miss Langley. However she hadn't expected any real probing.

"A minor family," she said quickly. "Younger son . . . never goes to London . . . And now, if you will excuse me, sir, I would like to retire."

He raised an eyebrow but made no comment. He merely gave a short nod.

* * *

Saybrook poured himself another brandy after Jane had left, then settled into a comfortable wing chair near the fire. Stretching out his long legs, he stared into the flames while letting the amber spirits warm his insides. Why was it he always seemed to feel so cold here? He looked at his glass. He was drinking more than was good for him, he mused. He should watch himself—but it seemed to be the only thing that dulled the pain.

He let his mind wander back over the day's events. What had possessed him to allow that impertinent slip of a governess to stay on rather than sending her packing without references. He shook his head. He had been furious, but had also felt a grudging admiration for the spirit and courage it took for her to speak, knowing full well that it meant instant dismissal. He had also known that her anger had stemmed from concern for Peter. For that he was sincerely grateful.

And she had been right. That he could not argue, he told himself with brutal honesty. He *had* been behaving dismally, no matter that there were . . . He took another deep swallow of brandy.

In any case, he wouldn't dismiss a servant for speaking the truth, no matter how much it stung. And then suddenly he nearly shouted with laughter—she had threatened to horsewhip him, the impudent chit! It was truly outside of enough.

Miss Jane Langley. Her story explained why her bearing and demeanor were unlike that of a simple farm girl. Still, he had the feeling there was more to the story than she had let on. His eyes fell half closed as he regarded the flames. But why was he even thinking of a sharp-tongued governess, one who seemed to make sparks fly whenever he got near her. It was well enough to know that Peter was in good hands. He could leave Highwood with a clear conscience.

Givens entered the room, then stopped short when he saw Saybrook was sprawled in a chair. "Your pardon, my lord. I didn't realize you were still up. Shall I stoke the fire for you?"

"No, Givens. You may retire. I shall see to things myself."

"But, sir," remonstrated the butler.

"I am perfectly capable of banking a fire and carrying my own candle upstairs." Saybrook smiled at the old retainer. "Off to bed with you, and that is an order."

"Yes, Mr. Edward," replied Givens fondly. "Though I daresay you should sleep yourself." He looked with concern at the glass in Saybrook's hand, making him feel as if he were seven years old again.

"I will," replied the marquess, though it was another few hours and glasses of brandy before he headed to his own chambers.

Chapter Five

Jane slipped into the stables and smiled a greeting at the young groom mucking out stalls.

"Mr. Henry 'as 'er all saddled up fer ye, miss," he piped.

A mist still lay over the fields. The early morning sun was not yet strong enough to penetrate its hazy whiteness and coolness hung in the air, though summer was quite finished. Dew clung to the grass and leaves, dampening the sounds of the birds and crickets.

Jane loved the stillness of this time of day, the feeling of peace and solitude. Almost more than anything else it was the luxury of being alone that she missed. As a servant, she had precious little time for herself. She was lucky that Henry seemed to understand this need of hers and made no objection to her riding early in the morning before anyone else was up.

Today she had her favorite mount, a spirited filly, full in the chest, who loved to run all out if given her head. It was all Jane could do to check her eagerness until they came out of the wooded trail and into rolling pastureland, where the ground was still redolent with the sweet smell of freshly cut hay. The clouds were beginning to break up and the scattered patches of blue promised a glorious day. Jane smiled as the filly tossed her head again, tugging impatiently at the reins.

"All right, Bodicea," she murmured. "Let's fly!"
Putting her heels to the horse's flanks, she let the animal
have its head.

The wind whipped at her face and hair. Jane felt like
shouting for the sheer pleasure of it. She bent low in the
saddle and urged her mount on. Faster, faster, the hooves
pounded in a staccato rhythm on the earth.

Suddenly she was aware of something odd. A new
sound had joined in, an accompanying pounding. Puzzled, she was about to pull up and look around for its
source when out of the corner of her eye she noticed a
black shape shooting up to her. Then an arm shot out,
grabbing her bridle and wrenching her filly to an easy
trot, then a walk.

"Are you all right?" snapped a by-now familiar voice.
She felt the sea green eyes looking her up and down—
seemingly satisfied that she was not injured, the voice
continued. "What in Devil's name do you think you are
doing riding such a horse. You could have been killed!
Has Henry no more sense than to allow you to . . ."

"The only danger, sir, was in your reckless grabbing at
a galloping horse," she interrupted. "I was in perfect
control."

Saybrook looked momentarily taken aback.

"And Henry knows perfectly well that I am capable of
riding her, or any other horse in your stable, so you
needn't ring a peal over head." Jane was furious that her
morning had been so rudely interrupted.

"It did not appear so," replied Saybrook stiffly. "I was
merely trying to prevent an accident."

"Well, what you have managed to do is ruin a lovely
morning. Besides," she added waspishly, "why you
should care if I choose to break my own neck is beyond
me."

"I don't. But it *is* my horse—and a valuable one at that."

Jane bit her lip. Once again she had forgotten herself. How absurd she must seem to him. She ventured a glance at his face to see how angry he was at her impertinence. It was impassive except for what she thought was a glint of amusement in his eyes.

All at once she saw the humor of the situation, too. "Of course. I forgot," she managed to say, trying to stiffle a giggle. It was no use. It really was too silly for words. Her hand flew to her mouth but she couldn't hold back. A peal of laughter filled the air.

Saybrook stared at her for a moment. Then he, too, began to laugh, softly at first, then a rich baritone sound that complemented hers.

After a minute or two, Jane managed to stop and wipe the tears from her eyes. "Oh, how ridiculous! I don't know why it is that you seem to bring out the worst in me, my lord. I apologize for my rudeness. I assure you that I do not start out intending to speak thus, it's just that . . ."

" . . . that my selfish, arrogant character is too much to bear," he finished.

Jane could feel the heat rising in her face. She lowered her eyes to the pommel of her saddle.

"I, too, apologize—for ruining your morning," he continued. "Perhaps we could start afresh. Since you appear to enjoy a gallop, Miss Langley, would you care to race to the far oak?"

Jane's head popped up. "Hardly a fair match," she said, eyeing the powerful flanks of his black stallion. "I suggest a ten-yard head start for my mount."

"Agreed."

She gathered her reins and coaxed the filly in line with Saybrook's stallion.

"At your pleasure," he called.

Jane touched her heels to the horse's side while at the same time urging it forward with her voice. Still full of energy, the filly bolted forward, elated to be given her head. Jane bent low over his streaming mane. She kept her hands soft and her seat firm. As the wind whipped around her she cursed her flapping skirts. If only she had a proper riding habit!

The oak was coming closer and closer. But then, on her right, moving almost effortlessly appeared the black stallion. For a moment they were abreast of each other and Jane noted that Saybrook was nearly one with the animal, so well did he ride. Then the two of them pulled ahead, beating Jane and her filly by a length.

Both horses shone with sweat and their riders slowed them to a walk. Jane, too, was breathless with exertion and elation.

"What a magnificent animal, sir!"

"Yes," replied Saybrook as he patted the horse's neck. "He's a Nonpareil, aren't you, Hero." There was a short pause. "And did you learn to ride like that from your squire as well?"

"Y . . . y . . . y . . . yes," stammered Jane. She thought quickly. "And we always had horses around the farm."

"I see. So you learned on . . . a plowhorse?" His tone was bantering but he looked at her quizzically.

"The squire had a few blood horses." She quickly changed the subject. "Do you race Hero?"

Saybrook gave a slight smile. He didn't press her further but followed her lead.

"No, I have not considered it."

"Well, I'm sure he would do handsomely at Newcastle."

Again he gave her a questioning look. "And how would you know that, Miss Langley?"

"Just from what I manage to read," she answered lamely, mentally kicking herself for being so stupid. The heat of the race must have affected her judgment. She stole a sideways glance to see if he was still studying her face. Thankfully, his attention was on the upcoming woods.

She couldn't help but notice how good he looked in his buckskins and topcoat. His long hair was tousled about his ears and collar, making him look younger, more carefree. His expression also seemed more relaxed. It was as if for the moment he was allowing himself to put aside his usual hauteur. A curious feeling squeezed at her stomach. She felt almost giddy. Then she shook her and looked away. So what if he was damnably attractive at times?

They rode along in silence for a time.

"Do you ride every morning?" asked Saybrook as they came to a narrow lane used by farm carts.

"It is before my duties with Peter begin," she said a bit defensively. "Henry did not think you would object . . ."

"Miss Langley, I would take it kindly if you would not regard a simple question as if I am trying to bite your head off—no doubt your assessment of my character is such that you feel it necessary, but I'm not quite the monster you think."

Jane hung her head in shame. "Yes, sir. That is, yes, I try to ride every morning."

"Have you taken out Agrippa?"

"Indeed not, my lord. I did not mean to imply earlier that Henry would let anyone ride your prime stallions . . ."

"I should think you would find him to your liking. Henry will have him ready tomorrow. I should like to hear what you think of him. Good day, Miss Langley."

They had reached the elm-lined drive leading to the manor house and he spurred forward at a sharp canter, leaving Jane speechless.

Never had she known a gentleman to offer one of his stallions to a lady, much less care about her opinion of its merits! Even those friends who knew she was a bruising rider were loath to admit she might know as much as they about horseflesh. So lost in thought did she become that it took Henry's cheery good morning for her to realize she had arrived back at the stables.

Later that afternoon, when lessons were finished, Peter rushed off to the stables to meet Saybrook for a ride through the southern part of the estate. The marquess was taking more and more interest in his ward and it showed in the boy's demeanor. There was a cheerfulness about him that had been missing before and his eyes no longer had that wary look.

With the remainder of the afternoon free, Jane decided to write a note to Mary in the privacy of her own room. It was way past due—she had no idea how the time had seemed to fly by! Her friend deserved a few words to let her know that things were all right, nothing that might give Jane away if others saw the note but enough to assure Mary that their plans had not gone astray.

Engrossed with the task of composing the letter in her head, she entered her room with nary a glance around and began rummaging around for some paper and ink in her bureau. Only when she went to sit on the bed did she notice the dress.

It was a riding habit of deep navy, outdated in fashion but of fine fabric and detailing—an obviously costly dress. Jane stared at it for a moment, unable to figure out where it had possibly come from or what it was doing in her room. She put aside her writing material and left to find Mrs. Fairchild.

In the hallway, the upstairs maid was sweeping the floor.

"Polly," questioned Jane, "there is a dress in my room that does not belong to me. Do you know what it is doing there?"

"Oh yes, Miss Jane. I was told to put it there. It's from the attics, I think."

More perplexed than ever, Jane kept up her search for the housekeeper.

Mrs. Fairchild was having her tea in a small study that served as her sitting room. Jane repeated her question concerning the dress.

"Oh yes, that. His lordship asked that I get a riding habit from the attic. It was his sister's—Miss Sarah's. Her things are stored up there."

"But why?" exclaimed Jane.

Mrs. Fairchild thought for a moment. "Well he did mention something about how if you meant to ride every day perhaps you shouldn't spook the horses with—I believe he put it—those ghastly flapping skirts."

Jane gritted her teeth. Infuriating man. Only he would be able to show some thoughtfulness, then color it with a casual insult. She had a good mind to tell him to take his dress to the devil!

Mrs. Fairchild was watching her face. "Is something wrong?"

"No, not at all. How very . . . thoughtful of Lord Saybrook."

"He always has been, you know, even as a boy. Not a tenant on his lands wants for warm clothing and enough food. Takes care of his own, he does."

"Well, *I'm* not his," she muttered.

"What was that, dear?"

"Nothing, nothing. Pardon me for interrupting your tea. I think I shall return to my room until supper."

"Enjoy the dress," called Mrs. Fairchild. "Mr. Edward thinks it should only need a little altering in the bodice."

Jane nearly choked in anger. How dare he scrutinize her thus! He must consider himself quite well acquainted with the female form to make such a comment. Well, she had heard not a whisper to indicate that he was one of those gentlemen who sought to dally with his servants— but if he thought a dress would sweeten her up . . . She slammed her door with vehemence. The sound was startling, even to herself, and she hoped no one else had overhead such a fit of pique.

She looked at the dress again. With a pang of guilt she realized she wanted to keep it very much. How wonderful it would be to ride properly decked out! Well, keep it she would, she decided as she fingered the soft material. And just let him try to claim any advantage of it. Her chin jutted forward. She almost looked forward to thanking him.

Her chance came later that evening. After reading to Peter, she came back downstairs to fetch a fresh candle for her room and passed the library. The door was half open and she could see Saybrook reading by the fire, his long legs stretched out to catch the flickering warmth. He had removed his coat and sat in his shirtsleeves, cravat loosened and hair falling low over his forehead. Impulsively, she knocked on the door—rather loudly it seemed to her own ears.

Saybrook called for her to enter without looking up from his book. Even as she approached the fire he didn't so much as turn his head. It was only when she cleared her throat in impatience that he raised his eyes from the pages.

"Yes, Miss Langley?" His face was expressionless, only the eyebrows slightly arched in question.

"I . . ." Jane was flustered by his quiet demeanor. If he had looked at all smug or had smirked knowingly, she would have verbally boxed his ears. But this . . .

"I . . ." she began again.

"Yes?"

"I wish to thank you for the riding habit. It was very . . . generous of you." The words came out sounding more stilted than she meant.

"Actually it was very selfish."

It was Jane's turn to look questioningly.

"Couldn't abide the sight of those flapping, drab skirts," he continued. "Likely to spook my horses and cause serious injury."

Jane felt a burn of indignation rise inside of her. "You don't approve of my dress?"

He looked her slowly up and down, pointedly taking in the shapeless mouse brown dress buttoned to the neck and the severe bun with nary a ringlet to soften the effect. Then satisfied that he'd seen enough, he began reading again. "Hideous," he murmured.

"It is proper dress for a governess," she retorted.

"Is it? Well, why those of your profession insist on dressing in such a dowdy, unflattering manner is no concern of mine."

"There are *reasons,* sir, that it is considered proper."

"No doubt." He still didn't look up. "But you needn't fear for your virtue in this house, I assure you."

Jane was left feeling she was coming out decidedly the worse in this encounter. Summoning what little dignity she had remaining, she turned with a swish of her skirts.

"Good night, sir. Let me not keep you from your reading—it appears most engrossing," she called as she
stalked from the room.

"Good night, Miss Langley."

It was only when the door closed rather firmly that
Saybrook permitted himself a broad grin.

Rain had been coming down in torrents for the past few
days. The mood in the schoolroom had been restless, for
both Jane and Peter disliked being cooped up inside. So
when Jane rose and saw that the downpour had finally
ceased, she was determined to venture out for a quick
ride, despite the fact that the day was still dark and over-
cast.

She threw a cloak over her habit and hurried down to
the stables.

Henry eyed the skies doubtfully. "You are likely to get
a soaking, miss."

"I shall make it short, I promise. And a little water
will not cause any harm. Besides, I must check the
millpond. I have noticed that it has a tendency to flood
during rains."

Sure enough, as she rode by the pond she noticed that
it looked dangerously high. She must find the steward
and tell him that he must send some men to open the
sluice gates. Turning her mount back toward home, she
set into a smart canter despite the mud. There really was
no time to waste if a flood was to be avoided.

She handed her reins to a waiting groom and started
back to the manor, composing a sharp lecture for Mr.
Fielding—wasn't it his job to keep an eye on potential
problems? He should have been aware of the danger . . .
Just as she came to the graveled drive she spotted a
group of workmen walking toward the fields. Deciding

that it may take her too much time to locate the steward at this hour, Jane took matters into her own hands.

"John," she called to the leader of the group, "you must take your men and go to the millpond to open the gates."

The man looked momentarily surprised, but then he nodded at her tone of command. "Yes, miss."

Satisfied, Jane entered the house.

Saybrook caught a glimpse of the scene from the morning room, where he was taking a cup of coffee and reading the paper. With a muffled oath, he slammed down his cup and raced outside. "Where are you men going?" he shouted.

They stopped in their tracks. The foreman turned to face him. "Why, my lord, Miss Langley told us to go open the sluice gates."

"Have you forgotten who gives orders here?" Saybrook's voice was icy.

The man stared at his boots. "No, my lord. It's just that recently . . ." He trailed off in confusion.

"Yes, I gather that. But in the future you will act on my word, or that of Mr. Fielding," he said less sharply. His temper was still sorely tried, but he regretted having vented it on those who were not to blame. "I have already taken care of the matter," he added. "You may return to the work you were doing before."

He turned on his heel and reentered the house. Brushing past a startled Glavin, he threw open the library door. "Send Miss Langley to me," he roared at the butler. "*At once!*"

When Jane entered the room, still attired in her damp habit, Saybrook was pacing up and down in front of his desk. "What in God's name did you think you were doing, ordering those men to the river?" he snapped.

"With the storm of the past few days, if they didn't attend to the sluices, one of the fields would be flooded. Your steward should have noticed . . ."

"If they had opened the gates, more than a field would have been harmed—I ordered some men to strengthen the bridge below the pond first thing this morning, *before* we were to open the sluices," stormed Saybrook. "If those men had done as you ordered, people would have been killed!"

Jane's mouth flew open. "I didn't know!"

"Forgive me for not informing you, Miss Langley," he replied acidly. "Somehow, I am under the strange delusion that *I* make the decisions at Highwood. Is that clear?" Jane knew he was absolutely right, but somehow that knowledge made her behave badly. Her chin shot out. "In this case, yes."

"Bloody hell," he muttered through gritted teeth. "Do I have your promise not to take estate matters into your own hands from now on?"

The chin stuck out even farther. She knew she was acting like a child but she couldn't help it. "Perhaps."

"What! Why you . . . you impudent . . ." Saybrook's temper, frayed by the fear for his men's safety, snapped. With lightning quickness he moved to Jane's side and before she could react grabbed her about the waist. Kicking a chair around to face him, he sat down and put her over his knee. Once, twice, three times in rapid succession his hand came down on her backside.

"Let me go, you . . . you beast!"

"If you insist on behaving like a spoiled brat, you shall be treated like one." She was struggling in his grasp and the feel of her soft stomach and thighs felt rather interesting on his legs. Though his temper was gone, he held her tight, ignoring the flailing of her fists. Finally she managed to free herself.

"How *dare* you treat me like that!" she cried as she straightened her dress. "No one has *ever* spanked me before!"

"A grave mistake." He regarded her calmly. "For I'm sure you have richly deserved it on more occasions than this."

"Oooohhh!" She was so angry that words eluded her. In frustration she stamped her foot.

At that, the corners of Saybrook's mouth twitched uncontrollably. In another moment he was laughing aloud.

"Oh, do give off," she snapped. But the absurdity of it all was clear to her as well. In spite of her pique, she found herself joining his laughter.

"I'm afraid I have behaved very badly, my lord," she said as she regained her composure. "I apologize for my actions and assure you that I shall refrain from giving orders which are rightfully yours to give. Is that satisfactory?"

"Do I hear correctly. Has Miss Langley admitted to error?"

"I should hope that I, too, have the grace to admit when I am wrong. And I would appreciate it if you would inform me of my defects of character in a less demonstrative manner."

Saybrook had risen from the chair and he inclined a slight bow in her direction. "Agreed." He paused for a bit. "And I would hope that if you feel something is amiss at Highwood you will bring it to my attention."

She looked at him in surprise. "Would you pay it any heed?" she challenged.

"I would be a fool not to. You have good sense and a discerning eye—you were right about the pond."

"But I am merely a woman."

"I fail to see what that has to do with having good sense and a discerning eye. Now, if you will excuse me, I must see how the men are coming."

He strode out of the library, leaving Jane with more than enough food for thought for the day.

Chapter Six

Jane picked up a pile of fragrant linens. "Are you sure?" asked Mrs. Fairchild. "You certainly aren't expected to do such work . . ."

"I don't mind, truly. Annie will have more than enough to catch up with when she returns." The laundry maid had been given time off to nurse a sick child and the week's wash sat neatly starched and folded, but needed to be put away. Jane had caught Mrs. Fairchild struggling with a mass of sheets and had promptly relieved the older woman of her burden.

"Peter is down at the stables bringing his horse a treat from the kitchen, so I'm quite at leisure." She smiled.

After climbing the stairs, she turned down a hallway into the wing of the house she had never entered before. One, two, three, four—she counted the doors and entered a small room with huge pine linen presses that served the bedrooms of the wings. She added her pile to the others stacked in the nearest one and carefully closed the door to keep the lavender scent of the sachets locked inside.

As she walked back, she took her time, glancing in through the open doors at the carved furniture and rich fabrics of the various rooms. Each had its own color palette and motif, yet all reflected a hand of restraint and elegance. Clearly someone with taste had overseen the decorating of Highwood. Who, she wondered?

As she passed a closed door, she found herself wondering what Saybrook's rooms looked like. Were they dark and overbearing or as pleasant as these? Did his bed have a canopy? Was it an heirloom four-poster—she caught herself with a start and nearly blushed. How improper to even think about! Besides, she was still out of sorts with him over his high-handed treatment of her— the nerve of him to actually spank her! It was probably a good thing that since that scene a few days ago she had barely seen him. . . . Suddenly, something caught her eye. She stopped abruptly, backed up a few steps, and entered a small conservatory whose tall leaded windows reminded her so much of her own home that she felt a catch in her throat. But it was the piano that had caught her eye. It was a grand one, gleaming ebony in the afternoon light, its keys beckoning.

Without thinking, she seated herself down and began to play. There was a pile of sheet music on the stand but she began from memory, her fingers alive with the pleasure of playing once again. She hadn't realized how much she had missed it. All sense of time was forgotten as she lost herself in the emotions of her favorite Mozart sonata. Finally, she came to the end and let out a sigh, drained yet happy from the demands of the music.

"That was exquisite."

The voice was hardly more than a whisper. Jane whirled around to see Saybrook leaning in the doorway.

"Oh," she gulped and made to jump up.

"No, please," he said. "Do you know the 'Sonata in G minor'?"

She shook her head. "It is still too difficult for me, especially the middle passage."

He came across the room swiftly and seated himself beside her. "That I cannot believe. It is certainly no more demanding than the piece you just played."

His fingers began to move over the keys, and Jane noticed how long and graceful they were. And as she listened to the notes, she became aware that they were also strong, and capable of great sensitivity. It was her turn to be amazed. She sat mesmerized until he finished.

"My lord, you play beautifully!" she whispered. "I never would have expected that a gentleman . . ." She faltered.

" . . . that a gentleman would play the piano?" he finished. His lips compressed in an expression of bitterness. "Yes, I know. It is not considered manly, so my father told me—many times."

"But it is wonderful! You have a real gift." Impulsively she covered his left hand, which still rested on the keys, with her own. Somehow, she wanted to brush away the hurt she saw in him. "As if anyone could question your . . ." She stopped dead. What in heaven's name was she doing? She snatched away her hand and covered her embarrassment with a cough.

"I must be getting back. Mrs. Fairchild must be wondering what's become of me."

Saybrook was staring at her with an unfathomable look on his face. As she tried to rise, his hand grasped her firmly by the elbow.

"I really must go, my lord," she whispered, not daring to meet his eyes.

"Enough of me," he said. "It is *you*, Miss Langley, I wish to discuss. Such as where you learned to play like that."

"I . . . I told you. I was educated with a squire's daughter . . ."

His grip tightened. "Do you take me for a gudgeon? What country squire has a music master such as that? What is his name. Where does he live?"

"It is none of your concern!" she cried.

"Indeed it is! You are employed to look after my ward. I have every right to know your background."

Jane's mind was a blur of panic. All the carefully re-hearsed lines were forgotten in the face of his steely gaze. Desperately she sought for something to say. All she could think of was the truth.

"Please, sir, I cannot tell you that." To her consternation, she felt tears in her eyes. "I assure you there is nothing in my background that would make me unfit to be Peter's governess. It's just that . . . ." She paused, wondering whether to go on. Saybrook's eyes had never left her and she knew he would demand more. "You see, I've run away from my father. I would prefer it if no one knows where I am from. I feel safer that way."

"Why?"

Jane took a deep breath. "He wished to force me into a marriage I did not want."

Saybrook's hand slipped from her arm. She was surprised to see his brow furrow and a look of pain cross his features. "One should be free to marry whom one chooses," he said slowly.

Though Jane was free from his grasp she made no move to leave. "That is a strange opinion for you to hold, sir. I thought Society expected those of your station to marry for . . . practical reasons."

He gave a bitter laugh. "You are correct. But that doesn't make it right."

She looked at him with sudden understanding. "You don't like having to do what's expected of you."

This time his laugh was real. "And neither, Miss Langley, do you."

There was a moment of silence.

"Perhaps I could speak to your father for you."

Jane's eyes widened in amazement at the offer. The idea was nothing short of intriguing—it would be an interesting match. However, she merely shook her head. "You do not know my father."

"And you, perhaps, do not realize how persuasive a title can be to a father."

Jane repressed a small smile. "I'm not sure it would matter in this case. But I thank you for your generous offer. It is truly most kind of you."

"You have only to ask if you reconsider."

This time he made no move to stop her as she rose. However he thrust his handkerchief in her hand. "Wipe your eyes before you go back. I am sorry for upsetting you. I shall not press you further on the matter," he said rather gently. "And please feel free to come play whenever you wish."

As Jane reached the door, she turned. "Sir, would it be all right with you if I teach Peter to play?"

Saybrook looked startled. "If he wishes . . ."

"I think it would be a splendid idea. And perhaps you might help him, too." She didn't miss the spark of interest in his eyes. "I know you have many more pressing matters to attend to since you spend so much of your time locked away in your library, but maybe you could spare an odd moment or two—I know Peter would be in raptures."

Saybrook thought of the long, lonely hours with the brandy bottle.

"Perhaps," he answered gruffly.

As Jane made her way slowly back to the main part of the house she reflected that she was not the only one hiding deep, painful secrets. Under the influence of the music, Saybrook had let his mask of icy hauteur slip, giving her a glimpse of a person vastly different from the one he normally presented to the world. Why did he wish to appear cold and unfeeling when he wasn't that way at all? she wondered. She had thought that men had all the freedom in the world to be whom they chose. A surge of empathy for him welled up within her. They were more alike than he knew!

She dabbed once more at her eyes with the heavy silk handkerchief to remove any last vestige of tears. It smelled faintly of bay rum and something else she couldn't put a name on—it sent a tingle up her spine. She fingered the large embroidered "S" at one of the corners, then carefully folded it and put it in her pocket.

The wrong note rang out loud and jarring.

"No, no, you must spread your fingers like this," corrected Jane as she positioned Peter's fingers on the keys. "Try it again."

This time the boy completed the simple tune without a mishap.

"Well done, Peter." She laughed.

A slow clapping made them both turn around.

"Yes, bravo." Saybrook smiled from where he was lounging against the doorway. "You've made great progress."

"Oh, Uncle Edward, listen to this. I can also play a sea chanty," cried Peter, and he began to pick out a simple melody, making only two or three mistakes.

"I see we have a prodigy in the making," said Saybrook as he came and sat down on a corner of the bench. "Have you learned this duet? It was the first piece my music master taught my sister and me." He showed the boy one part, then began to play his own melody.

Peter laughed in delight. "Oh, that's ripping. Can we do it again?"

Jane had slipped off the bench to make room for the marquess and now stood watching the two dark heads bent over the keyboard. A warm smile stole across her face. Saybrook looked up for a moment and caught her look. He smiled back at her before returning his attention to the boy and the music.

Jane noted how some of the small lines of worry around his eyes had been erased, how he looked even more handsome now that the look of cold boredom had been replaced by sunnier emotions.

"Excuse me, my lord." Glavin stood in the doorway. "Cook sends word that supper is ready."

"Thank you. Tell her we are coming."

"Sir, just one more time," coaxed Peter.

Saybrook grabbed the boy around the waist like a sack of grain, setting off a fit of giggles. "Enough, brat." He laughed. "Cook will ring a peal over our heads if we ruin her dishes."

"Tomorrow then," begged Peter. "Say we can do it tomorrow."

Saybrook rolled his eyes at Jane.

She had to suppress a fit of giggles herself. "It seems, sir, you have opened Pandora's box . . ."

"Who's Pandora," demanded the boy. "There's no one in the house by that name. Is it a special box? Can I see it?"

"We are just getting to mythology," said Jane to Saybrook. Then to Peter she added, "And no, Peter, there isn't anyone named Pandora here and there isn't any real box. It is a type of fable that we shall learn about soon in our lessons."

"Oh," said the boy, sounding a bit disappointed. He thought for a second. "Then how can Uncle Edward open it?"

Saybrook's eyes flashed with mirth. "Yes, Miss Langley. How is that?"

"Beast," she hissed. "Peter, it's rather like the stories Reverend Burke tells in church. The stories teach us lessons about life. Well, Pandora and her box is a story which we shall learn about. And there is a moral to it as well."

"I don't think I will like that story—Reverend Burke is boring."

"Peter," warned Jane.

"Yes, miss," the boy sighed. "Don't speak ill of your elders."

Saybrook threw back his head with a peal of laughter. "Good Lord, I wouldn't be seven again for all the tea in China!"

"Then try not to act like it," she retorted in a low voice as she walked past him into the dining room.

Saybrook was seated at the head of the table with Jane to his right and Peter to his left. It was an arrangement which had only begun very recently, but Jane noted that it had been good for all concerned. It must have been very austere and lonely for the marquess to take his meals all by himself in the cavernous room night after night. So when he tentatively had suggested that it might be good for Peter to become accustomed to an adult table she had enthusiastically endorsed the plan. The boy was delighted with the change and had lost nearly all his shyness around his uncle. In fact, she could see the bond between the two of them growing stronger every day. And just the other day she had realized with a start that the marquess had been here for weeks and showed no sign of leaving.

She, too, had to admit that it was pleasant to have stimulating company at meals. Why, she even found herself looking forward to the verbal sparring that took place with Saybrook each evening.

"What do you think about the latest news of Wellington's movements in Spain?" she asked after the soup was served. She was curious as to his views on military tactics.

Saybrook raised an eyebrow at her. "And how do you know anything about Wellington?" he inquired.

"I read the same papers as you—after you have finished with them of course. Glavin puts them aside for me each night."

"I thought it was only proper for ladies to read about fashion and the betrothal notices."

Jane felt her temper rising. Why was it men assumed no woman had a brain—or could possibly use one if she had.

"No doubt you do." Her voice had an edge to it. "But then, I am not a lady, remember? No doubt you feel that ladies would be incapable of comprehending anything more demanding than the newest way to set a piece of lace or the latest *on-dit*. Why, I'm sure your ideal of a lady is sweet, biddable, and wouldn't dream of having an opinion about anything!"

The marquess nearly choked on his soup. He lay down his spoon slowly. "No, Miss Langley. I have no interest in vapid, uninteresting ladies, for such is what you describe."

Jane smiled to herself, thinking she had caught him out on this exchange. "Well then you must be hard-pressed to have an interesting time with the ladies."

A glint of amusement lit his eyes. "On the contrary, Miss Langley. But then again, perhaps it is because the ladies I know are proficient in arts other than conversation."

Jane's face flooded with color. She was about to take him to task for his utter lack of propriety when she noticed Peter's rapt face taking in the conversation. She set her jaw and put down her own spoon in stony silence.

"Now, about Wellington . . ." Saybrook continued as if nothing awkward had happened and launched into a detailed and lengthy assessment of the Spanish situation.

Despite her resolve to ignore him for the rest of the meal, she couldn't help being drawn into the discussion, disagreeing with him on some points, nodding in vigorous approval for others. She had just finished explaining why she thought the supply lines should be changed for the Peninsula campaign when she noticed that the last plates had been cleared away and a bottle of brandy had been placed by the marquess's side. How long had he been waiting for her and Peter to withdraw?

"Oh dear," she trailed off. "I'm afraid I've gotten carried away. Peter, come along to the drawing room. Forgive me, sir, for keeping you."

"Peter, go along and set up the chess board—you might care to practice your openings," said Saybrook. He turned to her. "Miss Langley, a moment."

She stopped midway in rising from her chair.

"I'm thoroughly enjoying our conversation. Why should you feel compelled to withdraw because you are a la . . . woman. Why not join me for a glass of brandy?"

Jane had never tasted brandy before. She knew she was being reckless but she wasn't going to back down from the challenge that seemed to come from his eyes.

"Why not." She smiled, hoping she sounded more sure of herself than she felt.

Saybrook poured two glasses and placed one squarely in front of her. He raised his own in toast.

"To Wellington."

Jane followed his example and took a large swallow. She nearly choked on the fiery spirits and had a hard time blinking back the tears that her strangled coughs were causing. Saybrook appeared not to notice as he continued the conversation, this time discussing the merits of the Allied cavalry. Every few minutes he would pause for another sip, and Jane felt compelled to match him.

Soon both glasses were empty.

"Would you like another?"

Jane's face felt on fire. "N . . . n . . . no, thank you."

His lips twitched.

Suddenly she felt hot all over. "You're making fun of me, aren't you, my lord? Making fun of . . . of a Miss Nobody who dares to try and exercise her own power of thought!"

"No, I am not," he replied quietly. "The conversation has been more intelligent and enjoyable than many I have had in my clubs—that's a compliment, Miss Langley, in case you are about to bite my head off. But I hope you have learned a lesson."

"And what is that? For someone who has been hired to give lessons in this house, I have, by *your* account, an inordinate amount of things to learn myself!" Jane hoped her voice didn't sound as wobbly as her knees felt.

"You should learn to count to ten," he countered. "Then perhaps you would learn not to act without thinking—at some point it might land you in serious trouble. Have you ever truly considered that?"

Jane bit her lip.

"And furthermore, it is not necessary to insist on doing everything a man does to make your point . . ."

"Men never get the point," she shot back.

He cocked his head to one side. "I hadn't thought of it overly much, but I suppose what you say has merit. Things aren't fair. However, aside from that, you have acted very foolishly."

Jane's chin came up and she opened her mouth to retort.

"Let me finish," he said.

Much to her own surprise, she closed her mouth and leaned back in her chair.

"Has no one ever told you not to drink spirits with a man, especially alone with a man?" he went on. "Who the Devil raised you? Did your father teach you nothing about your own safety, not to speak of propriety? Why, many employers would now have you lying across this table with your skirts up over your head. And there would be nothing—especially in the rather woozy state you are no doubt in—you could do about it!"

Jane's mouth dropped in an O of shock.

"Yes, you should be shocked," he said roughly.

Jane shrunk even further back in her chair. Why every time he decided to give her a set-down did he have to be right! Both her father and Thomas had cautioned her on much the same thing, though a bit more delicately. She should by all rights acknowledge her folly and thank him for his advice, but the brandy had made her reckless. Instead of contrite words, she blurted out, "Why aren't you?"

He looked at her with a strange expression. "I don't dally with my help," he answered coldly.

Jane felt a tightening in her stomach. She should be relieved, but . . .

"Peter is waiting for you," he added. "And ring for the footman to bring some water to the drawing room—you will feel better when you drink a glass."

Jane left the room in a whirl of conflicting emotions. She didn't know whether to be angry or appreciative, insulted or intrigued. Things were not as black and white as she had first supposed with Lord Saybrook. She wished she could understand him—and perhaps herself—better.

Saybrook pushed his chair back and stretched his long legs out in front of him. He swirled the brandy absently as he stared at the massive oak table. What in Devil's name had prompted him to say such an improper thing? She was so interesting to talk to that it was easy to forget she was only a green girl of barely twenty, innocent of the cynical mores of the *ton*. Sighing, he took a long sip of his drink. It was wicked of him, but he did enjoy goading Miss Langley to anger—not that it took much! Her sapphire eyes lit up so intensely, her chin jutted out in such a beguiling way. Why, she looked more than just plain, even with her hair pulled back in such a severe, unbecoming way.

He found himself wondering just what her figure was like underneath the shapeless, oversized dresses she wore. Were her breasts as firm and shapely as they sometimes seemed through the coarse material? And was her waist as slim as it appeared in her riding habit? What would her willowy form look like in a ball gown, with her shoulders bared. His eyes strayed back to the table . . . Good God, what was he thinking!

He slammed the glass down and stalked out of the room.

Another rainy day. Jane watched the drops trace long, spindly patterns down the glass panes as she sat before the piano. She had felt strangely out of sorts since the evening before. Perhaps it was the result of the brandy, but she didn't think so. It was just as well that Peter had run off to the stables to help the under groom polish tack, leaving her with a free hour.

She thumbed restlessly through a sheaf of music but nothing appealed to her. Finally she settled on a waltz. Perhaps its lilting melody would serve to lift her spirits. Her fingers started slowly, grudgingly, picking up the tempo as she went along. Indeed, it was hard to remain blue-deviled while playing such a piece.

So caught up was she in the music that she was unaware of Saybrook until he leaned casually over the piano, his elbows resting on the polished wood. Her fingers came to a stop. He reached down and began playing where she had left off.

"Have you ever waltzed?" he asked, a glint of amusement in his eyes.

"Now what do you think, my lord?" she answered evasively. "Though it must be rather fun." She thought longingly of the few dances she had been allowed to have after being approved by the Patronesses at Almack's.

"So it is." He kept playing. "Would you care to try?"

"Good heavens, of course not. It would not be proper!"

"Ah, haven't been approved by the Dragons at Almack's?" he teased. "No matter. The rules are always more relaxed at a country home. Come, I hadn't thought you so poor-spirited as to be afraid of trying something new."

"I'm not afraid," she mumbled, turning away from him.

"Good!"

He stopped playing but kept humming the tune in his rich baritone. Taking her by the elbow, he guided her out to the middle of the floor.

"Now put your hand on my shoulder like this," he said as his arm slipped around her waist. The steps are rather simple—just follow me."

He began humming again, his mouth close to her ear. She could feel the heat from his chest against hers, and the light pressure of his hand on the small of her back. He moved with a natural grace that made the dance seem effortless. Their steps flowed together as if they were one. She relaxed, letting herself draw closer to him.

Gradually he picked up the tempo and they swirled around the room. As if by magic, she could hear violins and piano, feel the layered silk of an evening gown, see the glittering of candles and crystal, smell the fragrance of orange blossoms and roses. When she chanced to look up, she found him smiling at her, a strange warmth in his sea green eyes. Shyly, she smiled back.

"Miss Jane! Uncle Edward! What are you doing?" Peter was standing in the doorway, watching them quizzically.

The spell was broken. Jane dropped her arm and pulled quickly away from the marquess. To her dismay, she could feel a deep blush creeping up her face.

"I am showing Miss Langley a waltz, imp," called Saybrook.

"Can I learn, too?"

Saybrook laughed. "When you are older."

"Are you ready for your lesson?" Jane smoothed at her skirts, trying to hide her embarrassment.

Peter scampered toward the instrument, but Saybrook took Jane's arm as she turned to go. He was still smiling. "You dance very well, Miss Langley. You must promise me the first waltz if by chance we meet at a ball."

"What fustian, sir. You are teasing me again."

"Indeed I am not. Come, give me your promise."

Instead of lessening, the color in her face deepened. "Oh, very well," she said, in order to make him release her arm. His touch was beginning to make her feel light-headed. "Though you are being quite ridiculous, you know."

Saybrook bowed to her in mock solemnity and left the room, the smile still on his lips.

Chapter Seven

Peter struggled with the heavy wicker basket, refusing Jane's help even though it knocked him in the shin with every step. "I'm not a baby," he insisted. "And a gentleman always carries a parcel for a lady."

Jane refrained from smiling and wondered where he had picked up that nugget of information.

"Very well," she said. "I think we have picked a glorious day for our outing."

The morning light was a rich gold, playing off the hints of color in the oaks and maples near the stables. The air was getting crisper, hinting at a change of season, but the cloudless sky promised that by noon the day would be deliciously warm. Jane had looked outdoors when she rose and suddenly had decided to declare a holiday from the schoolroom. Instead, they would take a long ride to visit the abbey ruins that lay not more than eight miles from Highwood. She had been meaning to take Peter there—it was a good history lesson, she had assured herself. And one should not waste such a glorious day!

As they reached the stables, Saybrook walked out from among the stalls. He had just returned from an early morning excursion with his steward to inspect a broken millstone. His coat of black superfine was draped over one arm and his cambric shirt was open at the neck, revealing a few curls of dark hair. The breeze had ruffled his locks and they fell rakishly across his forehead. Jane couldn't help but notice the way the light filtered through the thin material of his shirt, outlining the broad shoulders and narrow waist. The shirt was neatly tucked into skintight breeches which were immaculate even though his Hessians were spattered with mud.

"Uncle Edward, Uncle Edward! We are going on a picnic. Look! Cook has packed this whole basket and I carried it all by myself."

"Well done, imp." Saybrook took the basket in one hand and swung the boy up on his shoulder. He fell in step with Jane. "A splendid day for a ride. Where do you go?"

"To Salston Abbey," she replied.

"Would you like to come, too?" chirped the boy.

Saybrook cocked an eye at Jane. "I haven't been invited."

"Of course you are more than welcome to join us, my lord, if you don't think you would be too bored." Her mood suddenly felt even lighter. "Cook has prepared more than enough food . . ."

"Oh please, sir!" added Peter, who seemed unwilling to unwind his small arms from around Saybrook's neck until he got a satisfactory answer. In consequence, the marquess's collar was twisted and the top few buttons of his shirt had been pulled undone.

"If you leave off strangling me, brat, I shall finish my business here and join you on the way. Hero could use a rousing gallop."

"Hooray!" cried the boy as he slid to the ground, half pulling Saybrook's shirt from his breeches.

Jane couldn't help giggling. "Let us be off, sir, while you are still in one piece."

He returned her grin and raised his eyes in mock apprehension. "Yes, I fear my valet will ring a peal over me, won't he?"

A groom brought out the horses and Saybrook helped Jane to mount, then handed her the basket.

"I hope Peter has not ruined your day," she said in a low voice. "If you are too busy . . ."

"On the contrary, Miss Langley." His eyes had an expression she couldn't fathom. "I look forward to a most pleasant day." He glanced at the fast-disappearing figure of Peter and his pony. "You had best be off, too, before he lands in some mischief."

As Jane urged her horse forward, she couldn't help but wonder why it was that her stomach suddenly was feeling all aflutter.

The marquess was as good as his word. Well before they reached the abbey the sound of galloping hooves announced the arrival of Hero and his master. As Saybrook reined the big stallion into an easy walk, Jane noticed that he, too, was carrying a basket. Surely Cook could not have sent more food! Her questioning glance went from it to Saybrook's face, but aside from a smug smile he ignored her look and began to chat blandly about the weather and the prospects of the coming harvest.

Peter was less patient. After several minutes he could no longer contain his curiosity.

"What have you got in the basket, Uncle Edward?"

"You shall see later."

"But I want to know *now.*"

"No."

The boy was silent for a bit. Then he spoke up again. "Miss Jane could make you tell me," he challenged.

"Miss Jane could do no such thing," answered Saybrook coolly. He turned a challenging gaze toward her.

He had never spoken her name before. Jane's stomach gave an odd little lurch—she didn't understand what was the matter with her today. For some reason she found it impossible to meet his look.

"Peter," she admonished, in order to hide her confusion, "you mustn't be impertinent to . . ."

"And just why do you think Miss Jane could make me tell you?" Saybrook asked the boy. Though his face was serious, the twinkle in his eyes gave hint that he was enjoying himself immensely. "I'm quite curious."

The boy thought for a moment. "Miss Jane has a way of looking at you that makes you feel you have to do what she says without any argument," he said. "And I heard Cook say so to Mrs. Fairchild as well. Mrs. Fairchild said yes, it seemed that any difficulty that arose, one had only to apply to Miss Jane and she would settle it because no one dared argue with her. Then she said . . ." The boy paused. "I think she said there was an air about Miss Jane, as if she was to the manner born—what air can be around Miss Jane that isn't around us?"

"Peter!" exclaimed Jane.

"How odd," remarked Saybrook dryly. "I was under the impression that I had something to do with running Highwood. What a relief to know it is in good hands."

"My lord." Jane faltered. "I don't know where he picks up such things . . . He must have misunderstood something he overheard . . . It is nonsense . . ." She stopped, utterly at a loss for words. Her face was flaming and her eyes went to Saybrook in mute appeal.

"Please, this is a silly conversation—let us forget it," she managed to say.

"Ah, the look!" replied Saybrook, trying to suppress his mirth. "I see I dare not disobey such a command."

"My lord, you are making fun of me."

The marquess gave a shout of laughter as he spurred Hero into a canter. "Peter," he called, "there is the abbey up ahead. Shall we race there?"

The two horses kicked up a cloud of dust, leaving Jane to settle her own swirling emotions as she made her own way toward the crumbling stone ruins.

Saybrook tethered their horses on a grassy knoll and took up both baskets. "I should like to show Peter the abbey before luncheon, if you don't mind, sir," said Jane. "It is his history lesson for the day."

"Of course."

They had entered an open courtyard, and though the walls were now no taller than an average man's chest they formed a shelter from the breeze. The sun had warmed the grass and gray stone, making it feel quite pleasant. Saybrook placed both the large hamper and his smaller basket down and unfolded a large blanket that had been tucked on top of Cook's repast.

"This seems a perfect spot." He turned a questioning look to Jane and she nodded her approval.

"Now, Peter, let us start with the main building. There is a fascinating story about it . . ." She took the boy's hand and led him away. Out of the corner of her eye she saw Saybrook take something from his basket and walk in an opposite direction. She thought she heard the sound of running water coming from somewhere over there, but as Peter was tugging at her hand, she quickly returned her attention to showing him around.

To her surprise, Saybrook joined them shortly thereafter. She hadn't expected him to show any interest in a tour of the ruins, but he fell in step with them, his hands clasped behind his back, his head slightly cocked as if attentive to her every word. In fact, she was acutely aware of his gaze, even with her back turned, as she explained to Peter the design of the buttresses in the transept of the ancient church.

As they strolled to examine some of the outbuildings Jane began to relate the part the abbey had played in the battle between Henry III and Simon de Montfort.

"Henry's son, Edward, had moved his men here to camp right alongside the abbey," began Jane.

"Edward was called Longshanks, you know, because he was so tall," interrupted Saybrook. "He was a superb horseman—in fact, that is how he escaped from de Montfort in the first place. Do you know that story?"

Peter shook his head, and Saybrook gave a brief but very lucid explanation of the conflict between the King of England and his brother-in-law, Simon de Montfort. The boy listened in rapt attention.

"Sorry," apologized Saybrook as he finished and looked over at Jane. "I broke in on you." The surprise was still so evident on her face that he added, "I did manage to learn a few things while at Oxford. History was a favorite of mine."

"Please." She smiled. "Do go on."

As she listened to him regale Peter with the exploits of long-ago heroes she couldn't help but think how he constantly surprised her. In moments such as these it was hard to believe there was a cold and unbearably proud side to him, the face that he wished the world to see. It seemed to her that when the mask slipped—which had been occurring with increasing frequency over the past few weeks—it revealed a sensitive, caring person. Even now, as he spoke to his ward, his features were alive with good spirits and his eyes held the warmth of summer rain. With his hair tousled by the wind and curling softly around his ears and neck he looked rather boyish and vulnerable—and even more handsome than ever.

Saybrook looked up to find her staring at him.

"Have I said something you disagree with? You must not hesitate to correct my facts. It has been a long time since I have been in a schoolroom."

Jane quickly lowered her eyes. "Not at all, my lord. I, too, have been entranced by your story. I feel I have been given a holiday from my duties. You best beware, 'else I ask you to consider adding tutoring history to your other responsibilities at Highwood." She kept her tone light and bantering, hoping that he would never guess her true thoughts.

They had walked on beyond the ruins of the buttery and sheds to where a stream flowed through a small copse of oaks.

"Oh, look," cried Peter and dashed to the edge of the water, where he began launching small sticks into the current.

"Mind your feet," called Jane. "I don't want you to catch a chill." She turned to Saybrook. "What is it about water and mud that attracts little boys like a flame does moths?" She laughed. "It will be a wonder if there is a clean spot of linen on his shirt when he is finished."

Saybrook chuckled. "I seem to remember doing exactly the same thing at his age."

"I can't imagine."

A look of genuine surprise came over his face. "Why is that?"

"Well, it is hard to imagine you unbending and having fun, my lord," she answered just to tease him.

"You think I'm stuffy?"

"Mmmm. High in the instep might be another way of putting it."

"Hmmph." The marquess snorted. "You are being impertinent, Miss Langley."

"And you are being—how did you put it?—stuffy, my lord. If you intend to tease, as you did earlier, you must expect to get it back."

He laughed heartily. "Touché, Miss Langley. Why is it that you, of anyone I know, is so capable of pointing out to me my faults."

"It was not meant as such," she said quietly. "It was meant as fun, sir. You aren't nearly so bad as you want people to think."

"A rare compliment indeed!" He was still smiling but had an odd look in his eyes. "On that note, what say you that we declare a truce for the rest of the glorious afternoon?"

"Very well." She turned to face him and was surprised to see that he was taking off his coat.

"Would you mind?" He grinned, handing her the garment. Before she could say a word he walked to the edge of the stream, bent down with Peter and began fashioning a boat of his own out of the broken branches lying around the bank.

"I shall lay out the luncheon," she called, and received a distracted wave of acknowledgement from Saybrook, though neither of them looked up from what they were doing.

Cook had been generous indeed. A roast chicken had been carefully wrapped, along with crusty rolls, pickles, thick wedges of Stilton, and fragrant apple pastries. A jug of fresh apple cider, still cool from the cellar, accompanied the food. Jane arranged everything on a low stone ledge then sat down on the blanket, enjoying the warmth of the sun. She lay back and closed her eyes, listening to the shouts and groans coming from down by the stream. It made her smile, and she could feel a warmth inside her even greater than the sunshine. What a lovely day, she mused, slipping into a dreamy state somewhere between sleep and wakefulness. In it she began to picture . . .

Peter's shouts brought her back to reality sometime later. She sat up quickly to see the boy running toward her, liberally spattered with mud and shirttails hanging willy-nilly from his pantaloons.

"We had a splendid race and my boat beat Uncle Edwards," he cried happily. "I'm starved! Did Cook pack enough to eat?"

"Look at you!" Jane smiled. "Congratulations, Admiral, but at least wipe your face and hands before you sit down to dine." She handed him a large linen napkin. "And sit here next to me in the sun, so you warm up."

"Have you another napkin?"

Jane looked up and began to laugh. Saybrook looked nearly as bad as the boy. A wide smear of mud stretched over the left thigh of his breeches and his boots were hopelessly water-stained.

"Dratted fallen tree." He winked. "Took me precious seconds to free my vessel, 'else it surely would have won, hands down."

"Uncle Edward was balancing on a fallen tree trunk when it snapped, and he nearly fell on his . . ."

"Funny, is it, brat?" He threw a playful cuff at the boy while seating himself on the blanket.

"Your bootmaker will no doubt be as pleased as Peter," remarked Jane as she handed him a napkin as well.

"Yes, they are ruined, no doubt," he replied, surveying the once-shining leather stretched out before him. "I shall have to send to Hoby for another pair—my valet would give notice if I attempted to appear in these anymore. . . . Ah, the sun feels nice, doesn't it?" He closed his eyes and threw back his head for a moment. "Your pardon," he added, "for appearing for a meal in such a state."

Jane smiled. "I think for today the rules of Society may be relaxed."

"Good!" From behind his back Saybrook pulled a slender green bottle. "I put this in the stream earlier to chill and it's ready now."

"What is it?" asked Jane.

"A bottle of Mosel wine—light, fruity, perfect for the occasion."

"I couldn't . . ."

"Yes, yes, I know. It wouldn't be proper." He mimicked her tone. "But the rules are suspended for today, remember?"

Without waiting for another word he uncorked the wine and poured two glasses. "To a lovely day. I thank you for inviting me."

"A lovely day," she repeated.

He was right. It was delicious. Soft, slightly sweet, and very heady.

Peter had been eying the food longingly. "Miss Jane, may we begin? I'm famished!"

"Oh, Peter, forgive us. Of course!" She put her glass down and fixed the boy a plate.

She passed one to Saybrook as well, then helped herself to Cook's repast. Soon the three of them were lost in a spirited conversation, so much so that Jane didn't notice Saybrook refilling her glass. What she did notice was the unconscious smile that crept onto the marquess's face as he watched Peter chatter happily throughout the meal. Whatever it was that normally hardened his features—and she had come to decide it was no mere haughtiness but a private pain she could not begin to fathom—it was gone in moments like this. She found herself wishing she could keep it at bay indefinitely, for his sake.

"Oh, look!" cried Peter, his eyes following a colorful monarch butterfly. He put aside his nearly empty plate and dashed after it.

"You have worked miracles," said Saybrook softly, his eyes still following the boy. "He has learned to be happy—you are an excellent teacher."

"Happiness is not something you can teach, my lord. It is a gift. And it is you who have given it to him."

He looked startled. "I?"

"Oh, yes." She knew it would be prudent to stop there, but the wine had made her even bolder than normal. "You have given him love. Of course it has been a gift to yourself as well."

"Indeed!"

"Once in a while you actually allow yourself to be happy, too."

His face changed. The faint lines on either side of his mouth hardened. "What makes you think I am un-happy?"

She considered his words. "At first, I believed you were as cold and unfeeling as you wish everyone to think," she answered frankly. "But now I know you are not. I see you with Peter." The wine must truly have loosened her tongue for she went on. "I wonder why it is that you won't allow yourself to be . . ."

"You are being impertinent again, Miss Langley." He cut her off, not unkindly, but firmly.

She was silent for a few moments, but something inside spurred her to continue. "I have been watching you with Peter. You truly like children. Don't you think of setting up your own nursery? You would be a good father."

Saybrook stared at her in surprise.

"Oh dear, forgive me, sir." This time she felt she had gone too far. "I should never have said such a thing, I know. I don't know why I cannot curb my tongue."

Saybrook's look turned to one of amusement. "It is of no matter. I find I am getting quite used to it. But I assure you, I have no intention of marrying. Ever."

Her curiosity was piqued. "Why is that? Don't you at least have a duty . . ."

"Duty be hanged. I cannot imagine myself leg-shackled to *any* lady of my acquaintance. Mamas are constantly thrusting their chits under my nose—there are those who simper and say what they imagine you want to hear, there are those whose faces light up like a banker's on hearing your rank and fortune—any of them will do whatever it takes to achieve their goal, whether it is lie, deceive . . . You have no idea what the ladies of my class are like. Marriage! I think not. I prefer female company that is . . . less demanding." He took a deep breath. "You, on the other hand, are different and to be admired, Miss Langley. *You,* at least, are deucedly honest. *You* are not capable of deceit."

Jane suddenly felt hollow inside. She hoped that her voice didn't betray the guilt she felt as she answered him.

"It seems a very cynical outlook, sir," she managed to stammer.

"Do I shock you? If you had experience in Society, you might understand of what I speak. It is not a pleasant thing to be looked at like . . ." He stopped, as if searching for words.

"Like a stallion at Tattersall's?" she suggested.

He gave a chuckle. "Well put."

Jane thought of her own experiences in Town. "I think I do understand what you are saying, sir. You are a romantic at heart. You wish to be loved for yourself, not for your money or your title."

His face became stony. "No, Miss Langley, you have the wrong of it. I am no romantic," he said bitterly. "I do not wish to be loved, or to love. I wish to be left alone."

She wondered what had caused such bitterness, but before she could say anything else, Peter came running back, breathless.

"It was too quick," he announced, flopping down next to Jane. She put her arm around his small shoulders and he snuggled closer, resting his head on her lap. Her fingers moved to brush the dark hair out of his eyes, the same sea green eyes as—a sudden realization swept over her. The same eyes. The same straight nose and chiseled cheekbones. The hands, so different in size yet similar in shape and grace of movement. She had seen a painting of the marquess's sister and her husband in the conservatory but it had never really registered until then. They were both blond, with hazel eyes, and the baron was rather short and stocky. Could it be that . . .

Out of the blue, Peter spoke up. With childlike directness he asked, "Why do you always wear your hair in such a tight bun?"

"Because it is proper for a governess."

"But why?" he persisted. "Lady Carew and her daughter don't. And neither does the vicar's wife. Cook says it is very severe."

"Peter! Haven't I told you that a gentleman never takes note of gossip, and he certainly doesn't repeat it."

Out of the corner of her eye she saw that Saybrook was grinning again.

"Severe," he repeated. "I quite agree with Cook."

"Please, sir, don't encourage him," she appealed.

"Can I see it down?" continued Peter.

She froze. "Certainly n—"

Saybrook smiled at her and motioned for her to take the pins out.

"Please," cajoled the boy.

Perhaps it was still the effect of the wine, but all of a sudden she relented. "Very well."

She began to remove the hairpins and her thick tresses cascaded down over her shoulders. The sunlight cut through the dullness of the walnut wash and picked out the golden highlights of her curls. Absently, her hand moved up to brush away a lock from her face.

"Ooooh, Miss Jane," said Peter. "Why, you are beautiful! Isn't she, Uncle Edward?"

"Indeed." The grin had been replaced by some more inscrutable expression.

"You see, Peter. A gentleman must always be polite," she said to mask her embarrassment. To her dismay she could feel the color mounting in her face, just like some schoolroom miss receiving her first compliment. She quickly began fumbling for the pins and twisting her hair back into a thick rope.

"Leave it down," murmured Saybrook.

Her hands paused.

"Just this afternoon. The rules, remember, are suspended." There was a strange, poignant appeal in his look, something that made her release the mass of curls.

"Just this afternoon."

He smiled again and she tried to ignore the fluttering she felt inside.

"When can I see what's inside your basket?" Peter had suddenly spied the mysterious bundle sitting on the ledge.

"Go ahead and look, brat."

"A kite! It's a kite! Will you show me how to fly it?"

Saybrook scrambled to his feet. "We must go out into the field where there are no trees." He turned to Jane, but she waved them both on their way.

"The two of you go along. I shall pack up everything here." What she really needed was a little time alone to sort through her tangled emotions.

The sun was beginning to set as they rode back toward Highwood. Peter wore an expression of complete bliss but Jane could tell by the way his chatter had died down and by the tilt of his shoulders that he was struggling to stay awake. Even she had to admit she was not unhappy to see the white limestone facade of the great house through the trees. She and Saybrook had spoken little on the way back, but it was a companionable silence, comfortable and easy as they exchanged smiles over some of Peter's more exuberant observations.

Though the grooms were waiting for them, it was Saybrook who reached up to help her from the saddle, his strong, lithe fingers around her waist, lifting her effortlessly. As Peter slid off his pony, it seemed as if he would keep going, right to the ground until Saybrook's arm shot out and caught him about the waist. Hoisting the boy to his shoulder, he remarked how it was time for imps to be in bed.

"I'm not tired," protested Peter as he wrapped his arm around the marquess's neck. "I don't want to go to bed. I don't want today to end."

Jane was walking alongside Saybrook, carrying the baskets. She reached up and ruffled the boy's hair. "There will be other days."

"As nice as this?"

"I certainly hope so."

From the drawing room window Mrs. Fairchild and Glavin watched them approach.

"Such a lovely picture they make, don't they? If only it was possible . . ." She sighed and let her words trail off.

Glavin nodded. "Haven't seen his lordship this happy since his mother was alive."

Jane went around to the kitchen entrance and handed the baskets to the scullery maid. She caught up with Saybrook in the main entrance hall, where the footmen were struggling to keep straight faces at the sight of the marquess, disheveled and mud-spattered, with a sleepy little boy entwined around his neck.

"My lord," called Jane as he began to climb the stairs, "let me take Peter to bed. You needn't . . ."

"I don't mind." He kept going, giving her no chance to argue.

She fell in step behind him, feeling a little grateful that she didn't, in fact, have to manage carrying the boy. Peter was fast asleep when Saybrook put him down on the bed and held him up while Jane unbuttoned his shirt and slipped his nightshirt over his head. She slid off his muddy pantaloons and shoes, then tucked him under the covers. Saybrook had lit the candle on the boy's nightstand. He guided her into the empty hallway and shut the door behind them.

"Do you care to sup tonight?" he inquired.

Jane shook her head. "No, I think I shall retire, too. It has been a long day."

He made no reply but walked—slowly, it seemed to her—by her side. His shoulders were so close to hers that she could feel the warmth from them. It made her think of how wide they had looked this morning, how the muscles had shown through the thin fabric of his shirt. And she thought as well of how the shirt had been open, revealing the tanned neck and the hint of dark curls on his chest. All at once, her stomach was aflutter and the warmth was coming not just from his presence but from deep within her.

They had reached the door to her room and Saybrook turned to face her. He was close, almost touching her.

"Thank you, Miss Langley, for a lovely day," he said softly, in barely more than a whisper. The candlelight played off his tousled hair and his eyes, which were fixed intently on her own with an expression that made her feel a bit dizzy.

"It was kind of you to come. It . . . made Peter very happy," she managed to stammer.

He nodded, but made no move to leave. Neither did he speak. He seemed to be lost in thought as he regarded the flickering candle.

"Good night, my lord." Jane's hand went hesitantly to the doorknob.

"Let your hair loose from now on," he said abruptly.

Her hand flew from the knob to where her hastily pinned locks hung in disarray around the nape of her neck. "Oh, sir! I couldn't. It wouldn't be at all proper."

"Perhaps not, but . . . please do it." His hand reached out and slowly brushed a tendril away from her cheek.

Jane nearly gasped aloud as his fingers, barely touching her skin, sent sparks throughout her whole being. As she breathed in, she was acutely aware of his scent, a mixture of bay rum, the faint spiciness of wine, and the earthy masculinity of exertion. She quickly averted her eyes to the floor, hoping that in that brief moment he hadn't read her desire for him to keep touching her.

His hand seemed to linger just an instant, then dropped to his side.

"Good night, Miss Langley." He turned and walked quickly down the hall.

* * *

Saybrook paced in front of the library fire, feeling much too agitated to take comfort in his favorite chair. He sighed and gave thanks that he hadn't encountered any of his servants, for his physical arousal was all too obvious. Miss Langley was affecting him like no other woman—not even Elizabeth. He took a long swallow of his brandy. They had both been so very young. What had he understood of love? On that point, at least, his father had been right.

Elizabeth had radiated a fragile innocence.

But Miss Langley! She radiated forthrightness, honesty, and a generosity of spirit. Yet there was also a passion lurking beneath her surface that inflamed his senses. She had ideas, opinions, feelings—he smiled ruefully at the thought of her chin jutting out when she was arguing, how her sapphire eyes flashed when she was angry or espousing some point of view. And tonight had he detected a flicker of some other emotion? He groaned aloud. When he had seen that look, he had barely been able to contain his desire. He had wanted to crush her to him, to cover those expressive lips with his own and explore her mouth with his tongue. His hands ached to feel the contours of her firm breasts, to see if her hips were as slender yet rounded as he imagined . . . The throbbing in his groin told him he must stop such thoughts or he would go mad!

How miserably he had failed a woman before. How could he ever be sure it wouldn't happen once more?

But he couldn't deny that Miss Langley made him feel alive again. For weeks there had been, almost unconsciously, a bond forming between them. More and more he was drawn to her presence. His pulse quickened when she was around. She had penetrated the hard shell he had carefully constructed around his emotions. She made him want to rant, to shout, to laugh, to scream in exasperation—and to love again. He had fought acknowledging what was happening, but today forced him to admit it. Yes. In spite of all his carefully crafted defenses, he had fallen in love, something he had vowed would never happen again.

As he watched the dying flames, he wondered what she would say if he asked her to marry him. Why, did she even care about him, or would it be only the title and the money that would sway her? Or would she think him mad? Society certainly would. But he didn't give a damn for their opinion. There was only one opinion he cared for, yet he was also terrified of what it would be.

What would it be if she knew the truth about him?

The answer frightened more than he could admit.

The stem of his glass snapped in his hand. He stared mutely at the shards of glass on the carpet. Flinging the remains of the glass into the fire, he collapsed into his armchair, burying his head in his hands. Broken dreams, a broken life. Could he ever come to terms with what had happened in the past? Could his life ever be whole again?

Jane somehow managed to walk to her bed. The blood was pounding in her ears and though the room was chilly, she felt a prickling heat at the back of her neck. She brought her hands to her cheeks and they were burning. Slowly, her pulse returned to normal and her breathing became less ragged. What was happening to her that the merest graze of his hand could affect her like this? Her hands dropped to her lap and she stared at them, amazed to see they were knotted together in a tight fist. She forced herself to take a few deep breaths.

The moon had just risen and its silvery light crept through her window, silhouetting a bouquet of flowers arranged in an old stoneware jug that sat on her dresser.

The same kind of flowers that she had clasped to her breast that first afternoon she had run into the marquess. It was funny, she thought with a soft smile, she had long ago ceased to think of him as proud and unfeeling—infuriating, yes, puzzling, too. But on seeing his relationship with Peter blossom, she knew of his depth of feelings, though he seemed to want the world to think otherwise.

And he was devilishly attractive! For some time now, every time he looked at her with those sea green eyes or flashed a lazy smile she had felt a curious twinge deep inside. She had found herself thinking what it would be like to entwine her hands in his long, silky locks, to feel his lips on hers—shocking, she chided herself. But with an ironic smile she finally admitted to herself that she had fallen head over heels for Edward Sebastian Fleetwood. She was in love with the maddening marquess.

How ironic, she thought bitterly. She hadn't thought it possible to want to give herself up to someone else and still be left whole—more than whole. And yet that was what she felt. Somehow she trusted he wouldn't trample her ideas, her spirit.

Saybrook had certain feelings for her as well; that she could sense. He had nearly spoken to her tonight, but what would he have said? A marquess could not think of offering a governess anything but a *carte-blanche*. The thought of him asking her to be his mistress made her feel ill.

Yet hadn't he made himself perfectly clear on how he felt about marriage, and females of their class in general? She bit her lip in distress. If she revealed her true identity, how could he feel anything but revulsion at her duplicity. Honesty. Forthrightness. That was why he held her in esteem. Certainly not for her looks or sweet disposition—she cringed at how many times she had verbally boxed his ears. He must think her a veritable shrew! A knot formed in the pit of her stomach. If he knew the truth, he would think her no different from all the scheming mamas and simpering young ladies in Town. She didn't think her pride could bear that.

Tears began to form as she wrestled with her thoughts. In a wild moment she thought of throwing on her cloak and leaving that instant. It was dangerous to remain. If he never knew the truth, at least he would never despise her, like all the other ladies of their class. But when she considered Peter, she knew she could not wound his innocent trust in such a cowardly manner.

Until she had sorted out just what to do, she must feign coolness toward Saybrook. She must never let him guess her true feelings.

Chapter Eight

The next morning Jane awoke feeling tired and empty. The mirror revealed hollows under her eyes that betrayed how little she had slept. At breakfast, Mrs. Fairchild had voiced her concern, but accepted the excuse of a headache. Jane refused to accede to the suggestion that she return to her bed and insisted she was certainly well enough to give Peter his lessons as usual.

Even the boy seemed to sense that something was troubling her, for he was quieter than usual and quick to follow her every request. As she sat with him, working out sums on a slate, a shadow loomed in the doorway.

"Uncle Edward!" exclaimed Peter, twisting around in his seat.

"Good morning, brat."

Saybrook had just returned from riding. His hair was windblown and his face ruddy from the wind, which only heightened the color in his eyes. He was smiling, though tiny lines around the corners of his mouth hinted at a lack of sleep. His wardrobe had recovered from the ravages of yesterday. A cravat was knotted perfectly at his throat. His buckskins were spotless and snug enough to reveal every curve and muscle. The boots were a different pair and shone brightly, despite a powdering of dust.

Jane studiously avoided meeting his gaze.

"I thought after lunch you might like to ride over to Smythe's farm with me. They are breaking some young horses."

The boy's eyes shone. "Oh, may I, Miss Jane?"

She nodded, still not looking at the marquess. "Yes, you may, provided you apply yourself to these sums for the next hour."

"I thought you might like to accompany us, too, Miss Langley," he added, giving a pointed look at her hair, wound in the usual tight bun.

"No, thank you, my lord. Not today," she answered, her voice cool and even. "Now, Peter, twelve plus fifteen . . ."

A puzzled look crossed Saybrook's face as he turned to go.

Jane was relieved to have the afternoon to herself. Her thoughts were still in a whirl of confusion. She was almost tempted to take Mrs. Fairchild's advice and slip back into bed. But instead she donned her oldest gown and took refuge in the gardens, toting a wicker basket and a pair of shears. The soft colors and delicate perfumes of the flowers always had a calming effect on her. She wandered through the paths, carefully clipping a lush bouquet from the profusion of plantings. The soft hum of the bees and the scent of lavender and roses made her feel better, if not happy, as she began cutting from a patch of gladiolas.

"Let me take that for you."

Jane felt a low thrill at the sound of the familiar, deep masculine voice. She turned in surprise, having not heard him approach, and dropped her shears in the process.

"I'm sorry I startled you." Saybrook bent to pick them up. "Still stealing the manor's flowers, I see." He grinned.

Jane didn't dare meet his eyes. Surely now that she had admitted her own feelings to herself, they would be more than obvious on her face.

"Thank you, my lord." She reached for the shears and turned quickly back to the flowers, studying them as if particularly engrossed by one of the stems.

Again a puzzled look came over Saybrook's features. "Is something the matter?" he asked quietly. "Have I given you any cause for . . . offense?"

Jane forced her voice to be steady. "How absurd, sir. How could a servant feel any such thing?"

He took her gently by the arm and turned her around. With a searching look he studied her averted face. "Look at me, Miss Langley. Something is wrong. I would hope that we have become good enough . . . friends that you will tell me what it is."

His hand was still on her arm, and she was achingly aware of it. Why, his very touch was making her tremble. As he sensed the tremors running through her, he pulled her closer in a protective manner. She should run, she told herself, and yet she was rooted to the ground. Against her conscious will, she found herself looking up at him.

His head came down slowly, and his lips met hers, gently but firmly. His mouth tasted warm and spicy, unlike any of the other kisses she had occasionally allowed a gentleman to steal. With those she had felt nothing but amusement, but now her senses were so overwhelmed that her knees might have given way if he hadn't slipped his arm around her waist and drawn her tightly to him.

His muscular thighs were crushed against her, the hard ridge between them pressed up against her. Instinctively she arched against him, drawing a soft groan as his mouth became more demanding. His tongue urged her mouth open, and when she responded, it thrust deep inside, tasting her, sending waves of fire through her every nerve.

It was her turn to moan. Without thinking, she dropped her shears and reached up to twine her fingers in his long hair, reveling in its thick silkiness. Their kiss deepened. Her own tongue hesitantly began its own explorations, surprised at how quickly it wanted more. Her whole being was aflame. There was a throbbing centered between her legs, sending hot waves of desire throughout her entire body.

Saybrook gave another hoarse groan. "Jane, Jane, do you know what you are doing to me?" he murmured as he released her mouth to trace a path with his lips down to the hollow of her neck. "God, I want you so badly, I want to make you . . ." He paused as if unable to say the next words.

Jane forced herself to come to her senses. "Stop it," she cried, pushing him roughly away. "How dare you!" Her worst fears seemed confirmed. "You want to make me what—your mistress? Just because I am a lowly governess, do you really think I would stoop so low as to tumble into your bed on command!"

The hurt showed in Saybrook's eyes. "Jane—Miss Langley—you misunderstood. I want . . ." He faltered. "That is, I assure you my intentions are honorable . . ."

Terrified of what he might say next, that she might be forced to admit her secret, Jane flung the most cutting words she could think of at him.

"And were your intentions honorable toward Peter's mother? What has become of her?"

Saybrook recoiled as if she had struck him. His face drained of all color and for a moment there was a look of infinite pain in his eyes before they became steely, impenetrable. He stood rigid, not a muscle twitching. It was all Jane could do to keep from throwing herself at his feet and begging forgiveness for wounding him so deeply, for she knew she had cut him to the very quick. But she told herself it was better that he should hate her rather than despise her.

There was a dead silence between them. Finally Jane spoke up in a voice hardly audible. "I will be leaving Highwood tomorrow morning. I think it best."

Saybrook's jaw clenched and unclenched as if he might speak. Instead, he spun on his heel and was gone.

Numbly, Jane gathered up her basket and shears. The array of freesia, lilies, and roses, a moment ago so gay and colorful to her eyes, now seemed lifeless—poor stems cut off to wither away. She walked slowly toward the house, hardly able to take in that this would be the last time she would tread that path.

As soon as she entered the kitchen, Mrs. Fairchild's hands flew to her face. "Goodness, child! Are you all right? Did something happen . . ."

"It's nothing, really," she lied. "My headache has come back, that's all." She put her basket on the table. "I shan't be down for supper."

Mrs. Fairchild nodded sympathetically. "You go right up to rest, my dear."

"I'll fix you a nice tissane," added Cook as she came round from the pantry.

At that moment Henry burst through the back door. "Is there something amiss here?" he inquired, a troubled look on his broad face as he surveyed the three of them.

Mrs. Fairchild and Cook exchanged concerned glances. "Why, not that we are aware of," answered the housekeeper. "What has happened?"

Henry shook his head in dismay. " 'Tis the master. Just now, he came to order Hero saddled—in a rare mood, I might add. Then, why, he pushed little Jimmy outta the way in order to mount." He paused, still shaking his head. "I've never known his lordship to touch a servant, not ever! And the look on his face—'twas enough to make your blood run cold." He looked around. "Something must have upset him something terrible."

Jane turned and left the room without a word. Mrs. Fairchild regarded her retreating form with a concerned look.

"Oh dear," whispered the older lady, twisting a handkerchief in her thin fingers. "Oh dear."

Jane sat on her bed, staring at the trunk that now awaited a footman to carry it down when the carriage arrived. A curt note had accompanied her supper tray, informing her that it would do so at eight in the morning. As she glanced out the window she saw that William Coachman was indeed pulling to a stop in front of the main entrance. She heaved a heavy sigh and collected her reticule as a knock sounded on the door. She would never see Highwood and its people again, and that stabbing thought nearly brought on the flood of tears that wouldn't come last night.

Last night had been beyond tears. She knew that she had to tell Peter herself. After she heard Mrs. Fairchild bring him upstairs to bed, she went to his room. Enfolding his small form in her arms, she haltingly explained that she must be leaving. No reasons of course, just simply that she must go. Instead of crying or begging her to stay, as she expected, he had reacted as inscrutably as his father. He merely stared at her with the same sea green eyes and held her hand very tightly. It had been infinitely worse than any words.

This morning the deep smudges under her eyes revealed that she had found but little sleep during the rest of the night. She paused to look in the small mirror one last time. Good-bye. Good-bye to Jane Langley.

Downstairs, Mrs. Fairchild dabbed at her eyes, then took Jane's hands in her own. "We shall all miss you very much, my dear," she said. "Promise that you will write to assure us you are well settled. I wish that you might reconsider . . ." She trailed off with a questioning look.

Jane shook her head. "It isn't possible," she said in a voice barely audible.

The housekeeper withdrew a large purse from her apron. "His lordship sends you your wages," she said hesitantly, holding it toward her.

Jane took it slowly, noting its weight. "Why it's far too much," she whispered. Opening it, she counted out exactly the amount that had originally been agreed upon. "That is all that is due me," she continued, and placed the purse on one of the carved hunt chests.

"But, Miss Jane," remonstrated Mrs. Fairchild, "you'll need funds to live on while you find a new position. And you'll need this, have you forgotten?" She placed a crisp envelope in Jane's hand. "A recommendation," she added. "You must have one in order to secure work."

"Oh. Yes, of course." She took the proffered letter and mechanically pushed it into her pocket. "I shall manage." Jane gave a forced smile.

Turning her head, she saw that the parlor maids, the scullery girls, and the footmen—even Cook and Glavin—had gathered in a subdued group. Quietly, one by one, they wished her well. At that, she finally felt the sting of tears.

"Thank you," she stammered, then fled outside.

William nodded a greeting to her as he opened the carriage door.

"Can you take me to Hawley where I might catch the mail coach?" she asked.

"His lordship says I am to take you wherever you wish to go, miss."

"Hawley will be fine."

"'Tain't safe for a female to travel unaccompanied," said William doggedly. "Let me take you wherever you're going."

Jane shook her head. She glanced around, feeling quite low that Peter hadn't come to say good-bye—but maybe it was better that way. She noticed that the curtains on the library were still drawn shut from the evening, but for a moment she thought she detected a slight movement there. She must stop that, she told herself. It was over.

She turned and quickly climbed into the carriage. William shut the door and climbed to his box. With a flick of the reins, he sent the team off down the drive at a brisk pace. Highwood was soon left behind.

Saybrook remained at the library window long after the coach had disappeared. What a mull he had made of trying to declare his feelings, he thought grimly. And what a gudgeon he had been to think she would have anything but disdain for him—she had guessed the truth and thought him no better than a hardened rake! Why, she had even thought that he had wanted to make her his mistress, so badly had he expressed himself. No, not badly, he corrected himself. Cowardly. He had been afraid to say the words, afraid of . . . Lord, he hadn't meant to kiss her, but she had seemed so . . . in need of comfort. And for a few perfect moments it had seemed that she had returned his feelings. How wrong he had been! Again.

And now she was gone. He turned his gaze to the purse now lying on his desk. She had refused it, as he had feared she would. How would she get along with so little money and no position? Would she be forced to return to her father and marry . . . A tight knot formed in his stomach. Well, if William carried out his orders, he would see to it that Miss Langley need not fear for anything, even though she would never willingly accept his help. In fact, if she knew of his plan her eyes would flash in indignation. . . .

He smiled crooked at the thought of those flashing eyes, that defiant chin. Lord, he would miss her. The reality of it was just beginning to hit him. Last night he had kept himself numbed with brandy to dull the searing pain. But now he faced the prospect of day after empty day. Only the thought of Peter—his son—kept the grief from being unbearable.

He slumped into his chair and buried his face in his hands. To his amazement, he felt tears on his cheeks. He hadn't cried since he was in short coats. Not at his mother's death, not even seven years ago. But he made no effort to stem their flow.

William handed Jane down from the carriage. The small inn's yard was quiet save for an ostler readying the change of horses for the mail coach. Not another passenger was in sight.

"I don't like it, miss," growled William. " 'Tis not fitting for you to travel alone. Why don't ye let me take ye where ye's going. It's what his lordship wants, and cor, I'd be glad of a little change of scene."

Jane smiled at him fondly. "Thank you for your concern, William, but I shall be fine. You needn't treat me like I was some fine lady."

"Well in my mind, ye is," he muttered under his breath. "At least let me go in and buy yer ticket for ye . . . Where to?"

Jane handed him a coin. "Turnbridge Wells."

"And then?"

"I . . . I shall decide that when I arrive," she answered. In fact, she had not decided just what to do. Should she return directly home or take refuge with the dowager dutchess, her grandmother, in London? That august lady, the only other person besides herself who was willing to stand up to the duke, would no doubt be willing to arrange a tête à tête with her father on neutral ground. She bit her lip. It was so hard to think about the future when all her thoughts were on the past.

William returned with her ticket and change. He took down her small trunk and stood doggedly by her side, even though she urged him to return to Highwood.

"A fine thing that would be," he exclaimed, looking offended that she had even suggested such a thing. "Te leave ye at the mercy of Lord knows what." He glanced around sourly, as if to confirm his notion that undesirables were lurking about.

Jane smiled and patted his arm, but secretly she was glad to have his company. She would be alone soon enough.

The mail coach lurched to a stop in front of the inn. One elderly woman clutching a large burlap sack to her chest got out, but aside from that there was no other movement within the coach. As the ostler began to switch the teams, the coachman clambered off his perch and rushed into the inn, no doubt to throw back a quick pint in the brief lull.

"Well, I best be getting ye in," remarked William as he swung her trunk up to where the luggage was tied.

Jane was thankful to see the coach was only half full. She settled herself between a mother with two small children and a thin cleric who gave her no more than a desultory glance before falling back to sleep with a loud snore.

"Ye take care now, miss." William poked his head in through the open door.

"Thank you for everything. Good-bye."

The door slammed. She had to fight back tears as she realized her last link to Highwood was now broken.

William watched the coach rumble away down the road. Miss Jane hadn't made it easy, but he wouldn't fail his lordship. Turnbridge Wells, it was, and from there he would have no difficulty in finding out her next destination. He motioned for an ostler to take the marquess's carriage into the stables. A saddle horse had already been hired from the landlord at the same time he had purchased Miss Langley's ticket. He should arrive at Turnbridge Wells well ahead of the coach. With a grim smile he swung into the saddle. He would take good care of the young miss—he remembered the look on Saybrook's face when he had received his orders—or it would be his own head on a platter.

Saybrook was roused from his misery by the sound of agitated voices in the hallway. "No, ma'am," exclaimed the parlor maid. "He told me he was going to be with his lordship. I thought . . ."

"Yes, of course," answered Mrs. Fairchild. "But I'm sure he isn't in there. Have you sent to the stables?"

"Yes, ma'am. No one has seen the lad. Oh, whatever shall we do?"

"Let me think." A note of concern had crept into her voice, and she stood in indecision before the nervous maid.

"What is the matter?" Saybrook stood in the library doorway. His voice was low and a bit hoarse.

Mrs. Fairchild turned to face him and nearly reached out her arms to comfort him, just as she had so many times when he was a small boy—he looked so drawn and saddened. "It's Peter," she managed to get out. "He is not to be found anywhere, and he told Mary early this morning that he was meeting you. You haven't . . ."

"No."

"Oh dear," she repeated. "No doubt he is around somewhere, but it is unlike him to be devious—I'm sorry we have disturbed you, Mr. Edward. We shall take care of it."

Saybrook's heart gave a lurch. Of course the boy would be devastated, too. In his own grief, he had been too selfish to realize that the boy would need comforting as well.

"I shall speak to Henry. If you are sure he is not somewhere in the house, I think we might need to begin looking around the estate." Saybrook sighed. He had a feeling he knew exactly what the boy was up to.

Jane looked out the window with unseeing eyes as the coach lurched along its way. It was badly sprung and even though the road had become less rutted since they had turned off of the country lanes, the passengers were still jostled together with uncomfortable frequency. She hardly noticed the bumps and heaves, so intent was she on holding back the flood of tears that threatened to burst forth at any moment.

The numbness was wearing away, giving way to a sense of loss so painful she felt she could hardly breathe. Her father had been right, she thought miserably. Her reckless behavior had finally ended in disaster, though of a different sort than he had imagined. True, her reputation would be in tatters if it became known she had lived at Highwood with the marquess in residence, but it was her heart that bore the damage now. Perhaps she should have told him of her masquerade and trusted that he would have understood. But instead, she had been too cowardly, too proud to risk facing his approbation.

She had let her impetuous tongue lash out and wound him beyond all bounds. She could see his face again in that moment—the instant of searing pain before his features froze into an expression so cold and hard that it chilled her even now. It was the last look she had seen of him before he had turned and left her. How he must hate her.

A single tear ran down her cheek. She dabbed at it quickly, hoping no one had seen it. However, no one was paying the least attention to her. She would give anything to take back those cruel words and the hurt she had caused. Her chin sank to her chest. Maybe it would be best she put aside her own notions and began to behave as Society expected. May be she should bow to her father's wishes and marry the proper Lord Hawthorne and spend her days being a dutiful wife. Maybe in time she would learn to be satisfied with that—if only she could forget a pair of flashing sea green eyes.

The coach rolled to a halt at a small inn and the rest of the passengers climbed out stiffly, grumbling heartily about how long it had been since the last stop. Jane had been unaware of how long they had been traveling. However as she climbed down herself it was clear from the angle of the sun that the time was well past noon. Though she hadn't yet eaten anything, she didn't feel in the least hungry and decided to use what little time she had to stretch her cramped limbs.

Ignoring the curious stares of the stable boys and ostlers, she began to walk slowly around the perimeter of the stableyard, still consumed by her own concerns. It took a moment to realize someone was calling her name. With a start she looked up to see Henry reining in his lathered horse, a look of worry creasing his lined features.

"Why, Henry! Whatever are you doing . . ." She suddenly noticed his expression. "Is something wrong?" she cried, her stomach tightening into a hard knot.

"It's Master Peter, Miss Jane," answered the groom. "He's gone missing and well, his lordship thought we had best check . . ."

"I would never . . ." She gasped.

"No, miss, of course not. But we think he hid in William's coach, and perhaps he did the same here."

He dismounted and walked quickly to the mail coach, casting an appraising eye over the outside baggage.

"If you will just hold Athena for me, miss, I'll climb up and make sure."

Jane stood holding the reins while Henry made his search. So much could happen to a small boy out alone. He could fall in a ditch and drown, or be grabbed by those unspeakable people who kidnapped children for slave labor. . . .

"Well, he ain't up here, as I suspected, but we had to be sure," said Henry as he climbed down. "Sorry to disturb you, miss . . . I, well, as I didn't get a chance to say good-bye earlier, I wish you very well. We shall miss you in the stables." The groom ducked his head and blushed at speaking so directly to someone of the opposite sex.

"I'm coming with you," said Jane suddenly.

"But, miss!" Henry looked even more discomforted. "I don't think . . . that is, his lordship didn't say anything about . . ."

Jane had already sprung into action. Ordering a startled ostler to remove her trunk from the coach, she hurried into the inn, returning a short time later with a satisfied look on her face. "The postboy is saddling a horse for me. It shan't be a minute."

"But, miss," he repeated. "You can't . . ." He waved his arms helplessly. "Besides, you ain't dressed for riding!"

"I shall manage quite well." Jane startled the ostlers even further by demanding a leg up and then tucking her voluminous skirts between her legs so she could ride astride. Their eyes widened at the sight of a very well turned pair of ankles set firmly in the stirrups.

"Come now, we must find him before nightfall."

The confused groom gave up and climbed into the saddle himself. He knew better than to argue with Miss Langley. "His lordship and the rest of the men have spread out from Hockam on the west side of the road. I'm to meet them by the fork and then we'll sweep down the east side. He can't have gotten very far on foot."

Jane nodded and put her heels to her horse.

They pushed their mounts hard, cutting across fields, jumping the stiles, galloping along the dusty lanes until they reached the appointed rendezvous. Henry shaded his eyes and surveyed the surrounding countryside. "We'd best wait here for the others."

"Perhaps I should start looking while you wait," she said, anxious to find the boy as well as to avoid a meeting with the marquess.

"I dunno, miss," said Henry slowly. Then he stopped as if his attention were caught by something beyond her shoulders.

Jane turned quickly. She, too, seemed to see a flash of movement far out in one of the fields to their left. She urged her mount over to the stone wall in order to have a better look, but now there appeared to be nothing.

"I think we had both better wait until his lordship arrives. He should be here shortly." The groom's nervousness was evident.

Sure enough a group of four riders appeared from around the bend in the road, perhaps a quarter of a mile away. Jane immediately recognized the black stallion in the lead. She took a deep breath and wondered how Saybrook would react to her presence. She turned her eyes back to the field, trying to compose herself for the meeting.

There it was again, a slight movement by a copse of elms. She kept staring and in another moment a slight figure came into view, that of a child. She heaved a sigh of relief and gave thanks that the boy was safe. As she began to call his name, another movement caught her eye, one quite close to the little figure trudging slowly along the edge of the field. The words froze in her throat as she saw the shape of a huge bull materialize from among the trees. It was trailing a broken rope from the ring in its nose, and its massive head swung from side to side as it approached the boy from behind.

"Peter!" she screamed. "Run for the trees!"

But even as she cried out, she could see that the boy would never be able to outrun the beast to safety. She jumped down from her horse and began to scramble over the wall, even though she knew she could never reach him in time. . . .

Suddenly a massive black shape hurtled over the stones close by her. In another moment, Hero was galloping across the field, Saybrook bent low over his neck. The marquess reined in the stallion just out of reach of the dangerous horns and flung himself from the saddle. The charging bull reached Peter seconds before Saybrook. It knocked the boy to the ground with a vicious blow from its head. As it rounded on the prostrate form, Saybrook scooped up the boy in one arm, then turned his own body to absorb the onslaught of the bull's next charge. He fell to his knees on impact, but managed to fend off the beast with one arm.

By this time, Henry and the three stable hands had ridden up and had formed a protective circle around the two figures. As they drove the bull away, Saybrook remained on his knees and laid the boy gently down on the ground.

"Peter!" Jane dropped to her knees beside Saybrook. The boy wasn't moving at all. She took one of his small hands and began chaffing it between her own. The marquess's breath was coming in ragged gulps and he hadn't taken his eyes from the small body before him.

"Dear God," he whispered, "is he . . ."

"No!" cried Jane. She had felt a faint pulse but the boy's face looked deathly pale and she had no idea how badly he was injured. "But we must get help!"

Saybrook seemed in a daze. He didn't react to her words and remained hunched over, one hand buried in his windblown hair.

"Henry!" shouted Jane. "Ride for Dr. Hastings and tell him to come to Highwood immediately."

"Yes, miss." Henry didn't wait for any word from the marquess but set his horse into a gallop.

"Georgie, Jack, and Tim, you must ride back to the manor and have Mrs. Fairchild prepare the Blue Room and get lots of hot water and clean linen ready." Jane turned to Saybrook. "Sir, you must take Peter up with you on Hero and get him home as quickly as possible."

She had already noticed that his arm was bent at a strange angle and feared it was broken. What other injuries he had sustained she dared not think about. Right now it was imperative to get him into a bed and a doctor's care.

Saybrook looked at her blankly. "Are you sure we should move him? I . . ."

"We must," she said firmly. "And quickly." As she spoke, her hand touched his shoulder lightly.

That seemed to rouse him from his state of shock. He picked up Peter's limp form and hurried to where Hero stood waiting.

"Let me hold him while you mount." As she took the boy, she noticed a smear of blood on Saybrook's hand. "You're hurt, my lord," she exclaimed.

"A scratch," he said faintly as he took the boy across his lap.

Jane watched him canter away, the motionless child cradled in his arms, looking so small, so vulnerable. She hurried to her own horse and mounted. As she urged it on toward Highwood, she began to pray.

Chapter Nine

The surroundings were familiar to her and she was able to cut through fields and woods to reach the manor house before Saybrook arrived with Peter. The servants were clustered near the main entrance, somber and awaiting further instructions concerning the young master. Mrs. Fairchild's eyes were already red from crying, but Jane noted everything she had ordered was in readiness. The Blue Room, the bedroom nearest the stairs was ready to receive the injured child. There was nothing to do but wait. Jane did so impatiently, pacing up and down the hall in silence. It was with great relief that she saw the doctor's curricle coming up the drive at a smart pace.

At the same time, Jane saw Hero approaching and she rushed to meet both of them. A groom led the curricle away and Dr. Hastings came to stand with her to await his patient. Jane had met him once before, when he had been summoned to treat Cook for a nasty fall she had taken down the cellar stairs. She had liked him at once and knew he had a fine reputation as a medical man. She slipped him a sidelong glance as she waited nervously, taking in his erect bearing, his close-cropped silver hair and whiskers and his clear hazel eyes which hinted at intelligence and a sense of humor. It was a reassuring picture. And he didn't disappoint her image. Even before

Saybrook had brought his tired horse to a halt, the doctor had quietly told two footmen to take Peter, instructing them exactly how to hold the injured child.

"This way, doctor," called Mrs. Fairchild.

As Jane turned to follow, she noticed that Saybrook dismounted stiffly and appeared to stumble as he started to walk to the house. But then the doctor was fast disappearing and she hurried to catch up.

At the doorway to the Blue Room, Dr. Hastings turned and raised his hand to the people behind him. "I will examine the boy alone, if you please," he announced firmly. "If I need assistance, I will call Miss"—his eyes searched for Jane—"Langley, is it?"

She nodded.

"Good. Your pardon, your lordship, but you and the others will only be in the way."

Saybrook stood at the head of the stairs, his arm clutching the newel post as if he were in need of physical support. He acknowledged the doctor's words with a brief nod.

The door closed.

"You may all go back to your duties." Jane spoke quietly to the two footmen and the anxious parlor maid who had accompanied them upstairs. Turning to Mrs. Fairchild, she continued. "Perhaps it would be best if we had some chairs brought . . ."

A cry of alarm interrupted her and she turned to see that Saybrook had fainted dead away onto the landing. With a sharp intake of breath, she rushed to where his crumpled form lay. As she gently turned him onto his back, his coat fell away from his side. Mrs. Fairchild screamed. His waistcoat was soaked in blood and a jagged gash in the cloth revealed an ugly wound at his ribs.

"Hot water, linen bandages, and basilicum powder! Now!" ordered Jane, hoping her tone would spur the older woman into action. "James, Charles, get his lordship to his bed."

Fortunately, the two footmen were sturdy fellows and able to lift the marquess without difficulty. His bedchamber was just across the hallway, and Jane hurried them in. She flung back the covers on the massive carved oak bed and had them lay the prostrate body on the fresh linen sheets.

"Ease his boots off, please," she called as she placed a pillow under his head. "One of you fetch a pair of scissors—and a bottle of brandy." All the while, her hand was unconsciously smoothing the dark hair back from his pale forehead.

Two maids arrived with a basin of hot water and a tray of medicines. Someone had thought to include a knife. Without waiting for the scissors, Jane began cutting away Saybrook's upper garments. She was not a total stranger to violent accidents and the sight of blood. At home she had sometimes accompanied Nanna, whose skills included nursing, on her visits to some of the surrounding tenants. Unbeknownst to her father, she had helped Nanna treat all manner of farm accidents, from broken limbs to severed fingers. It was hardly proper for a young lady of refinement, but she had felt useful.

Even so, she blanched and felt faint herself as she got his shirt off and saw the deep wound between his ribs. With trembling hands, she took a clean cloth and sponged the blood and gore from his chest. The bleeding had slowed considerably and she prayed that he had not lost too much blood. The very idea spurred her to work faster. She folded a length of linen into a soft pad and covered the wound, applying a good amount of pressure with the heel of her hand. After a few minutes, she took it away and satisfied that the flow was stanched, doused the jagged gash with a liberal amount of basilicum powder.

"James, lift his shoulders—carefully, now."

As the footman eased Saybrook up, Jane made another pad and wrapped it in place with a long length of bandage. She glanced around the spacious room, taking in the elegant dressing table and tasteful furnishings until her eye came to a large dresser. "Find me a clean shirt, Mary," she said to one of the maids, who knew exactly which drawer to open.

Jane slipped the garment around Saybrook's arms, leaving it open in front, then motioned for the footmen to ease him back down on the pillow. The white linen sheets accentuated the pallor of his skin underneath his light tan. Now that she had a moment to think, Jane felt afraid. She grasped his wrist, seeking a pulse. It was there, but weak, erratic.

"One of you knock on the Blue Room door and let the doctor know he is needed in here, too, as soon as he is done with Peter. The rest of you may go."

Her hand had kept hold of Saybrook's, the fingers slipping from the wrist to entwine with his senseless ones. They were cold as marble. She pressed her lips together. Dear God, she thought, he cannot . . .

Saybrook's eyes fluttered open. "Peter . . . ?" he whispered faintly.

Jane grasped his hand tighter. "The doctor is with him now."

He made a movement as if to rise but sunk back with an involuntary gasp. Beads of sweat formed on his forehead and his eyes narrowed with pain. Jane bent close to his head. "You mustn't try to move, sir," she whispered as she sponged his face with a clean cloth. "I shall take care of Peter—I promise you I will."

Saybrook tried to speak again, yet she couldn't make out his words. The effort proved too much for his waning strength and he lapsed back into unconsciousness.

"I see we have another patient."

Jane rose quickly, hoping the doctor wouldn't notice the tears in her eyes, and stepped back from the edge of the bed to allow him room. He threw back the open shirt and nodded in approval at Jane's bandage.

"A good job, Miss Langley. Do you have experience in nursing?"

"A little, sir."

"Well, it seems we shall need it." He pulled a chair closer and opened his black bag. "I shall have to remove your handiwork so that I may examine the wound . . ." His voice trailed off as he began to work. With a deft snip of his scissors, he removed the bandages. His brow furrowed at the sight of the ripped flesh. "Nasty," he muttered as he bent low to listen to Saybrook's shallow breathing and to probe gently around his side.

Jane clenched her hands together, unaware that her nails were drawing blood.

"Well," announced Dr. Hastings as he straightened up, "the horn appears to have missed the lung. I think two of the ribs are broken, so he will have to be kept quite still so they don't cause any damage. He is lucky."

Jane let her breath out slowly.

"However," continued the doctor, "it is not the wound itself that concerns me most, it is the danger of infection. The next twenty-four hours are critical. If a fever develops, we shall have reason to worry."

"I will do anything that is necessary," said Jane.

He nodded. "I believe he is in good hands." Reaching into his black bag he withdrew an amber bottle and placed it on the night table. "Tincture of laudanum. He will be in great pain if he wakes during the night. Try to

give him six drops in a glass of water every three hours."
He also placed a jar of salve next to it. "The bandage
should be changed every few hours and this should be
applied to the wound." There was a pause as he looked
searchingly at Jane's face. "Are you sure you don't want
me to hire a woman from the village who is experienced
in the sickroom?"

"No!" Jane hoped she didn't sound too shrill. "I
should rather do it myself, truly." She took a deep
breath. "And Peter?"

The doctor's look of concern didn't lessen as he re-
bandaged Saybrook's side. "I have set his broken arm,
but he has not regained consciousness. Head injuries are
very difficult to diagnose. Hard as it may sound, we
must simply wait and see. He may come round in an
hour, or a week or . . ."

"I see."

"You must send for me at any time if there is a
change. Otherwise, I shall call first thing in the morning.
And you must allow someone to help you." He regarded
the hollows under her eyes with concern. "Or else I shall
have three patients on my hands." He reached out a hand
to touch her shoulder and flashed a smile of encourage-
ment. "It shall all come right, miss. Good day."

"Thank you, Dr. Hastings."

Jane sunk into the chair the doctor had vacated. For a
moment she was assailed by an overwhelming sense of
despair. But then she set it aside, her jaw set in defiance
of the odds. "I won't let them go," she whispered to the
darkened room. "I won't!"

"Miss Jane?" A candle flickered in the darkness and
Jane snapped her head upright.

"You must take a bite to eat, my dear, and lie down for
a proper sleep. I shall sit with his lordship while you

do." Mrs. Fairchild hovered by her chair with a tray of food sent up by Cook.

"No, I'm awake—I must have just dozed off for a bit." Jane straightened slightly in the chair and looked at Saybrook. He was still sleeping, though his breathing sounded even more erratic. She reached over to feel his forehead. "Oh dear, he feels so hot. Do you think so, too?"

Mrs. Fairchild touched his brow. "Yes, it does seem warm. But come, I can do that," she added as she watched Jane sponge his face with cool water. She waited for a minute, then placed the tray on the night table with a sigh. "At least keep up your strength."

Jane smiled. "I shall, as soon as I check on Peter."

Mrs. Fairchild followed her from the room. "Mary is with him now. She knows to call you if anything changes."

"I know, but I want to see him myself."

Peter looked almost lost in the huge four-poster bed, his tiny form a mere smudge on the snowy sheets. His splinted arm lay outside the coverlet across his chest, which rose and fell with reassuring regularity. But still he had shown no signs of regaining consciousness.

"At least he shows no sign of fever." murmured Jane.

"No, Miss Jane, he's been right comfortable, if only he'd open his eyes."

Jane's hand caressed his cheek. "We must be patient—and pray."

Saybrook was tossing feverishly when Jane and Mrs. Fairchild returned to his room, his arm thrashing about at the covers, his breathing coming in ragged gasps. He was burning to the touch and Jane was gripped with a stabbing fear.

"Send for Dr. Hastings!" she cried as she lifted his head and put the glass of laudanum-laced water to his parched lips. He managed to swallow some of the liquid. After a few minutes it seemed to ease some of the discomfort and he became quieter. Jane took the opportunity to change the bandage, noting with alarm that the edges of the wound looked even more red and inflamed.

The shirt he was wearing was soaked with sweat so she stripped it off. As she unfolded a fresh one she couldn't help but be aware of his broad, muscular chest, the chiseled contour of his stomach, and the intriguing curls of dark hair, both across his breast and at his narrow hips, where they disappeared into the top of his breeches.

She had never seen a man so undressed before. There was a stirring deep inside at his rampant masculinity. Her hand lingered on his chest, brushing lightly over his undamaged ribs to the hollow of his stomach, where it rested just for a moment. She found herself wondering what it would have been like if she had accepted his *carte-blanche*. She could have been lying in these very sheets with his arms around her, his lean, hard body pressed tight to hers. A part of her longed to experience the strength of his arms and the fire of his kisses. She thought back to his kiss. Yes, she wanted more. A deep sigh escaped her lips. But she wanted more than just his passion. She wanted his love.

Saybrook began talking in his sleep, mostly unintelligible mutterings but occasionally a discernible word.

"No!" A gasp. "You mustn't!"

Jane touched his cheek. "It's all right, sir," she whispered.

"Father!" he groaned. "No!" He began tossing so violently that she could hardly hold his shoulders down. "No! No!" Then quite softly, "Jane."

"I'm here, sir. I won't leave you."

The tension seemed to drain from his body and he fell into a fitful sleep.

Dr. Hastings finally arrived. After a quick examination, he rose, shaking his head slightly. "It is as I feared. The fever has taken hold and we can only hope that his constitution proves strong enough to weather it." He looked at the frightened faces of Jane and Mrs. Fairchild as he reached into his bag and took out a bottle of medicine. "You must try to get him to swallow a dose of this every two hours. It is of utmost importance. Now shall I send a woman from the village?"

Jane shook her head doggedly.

The doctor regarded the dark circles under her eyes, then the determined thrust of her jaw. "Very well, then. I shall call again in the morning."

Jane sat upright in the chair, rubbing the sleep—what little there had been—from her eyes. The fever had been going on for over two days. At times it raged, forcing her to call for assistance in holding the writhing marquess to his bed. Then there were periods when it seemed to slacken, allowing him some fitful rest. She had managed to get the medicine down him, but she was beginning to doubt its efficacy. With each visit, the doctor merely pursed his lips and muttered that they must wait, that the climax would come soon when the fever either broke or . . .

Jane splashed some water on her drawn face. She was tired of waiting. She felt so helpless watching him suffer so. Perhaps Dr. Hastings wasn't as skilled as they thought. Perhaps they should send to London for a specialist? A quick glance toward the bed showed that Saybrook's face was more pallid than ever, and he seemed smaller, as if his ravaged body were wasting away in front of her. At least, for the moment, he was resting quietly.

"Miss Jane!" Mary hurried into the room. "It's Master Peter! He's opened his eyes. And he spoke! He asked for you."

Jane rushed to the boy's chamber.

"Miss Jane, I'm thirsty." He tried to throw his arms around her neck. "Oh! And my arm hurts!"

"Yes, I know, love," she said as she settled the broken limb. "You've been a very brave boy but now you must keep still so your arm can mend." She motioned for Mary to pour a glass of water, then added three drops of laudanum, as Dr. Hastings had advised. "Now drink this and you'll feel better."

Peter took a sip and made a face. "It tastes awful. I don't want it."

"Your uncle has to drink it, too, and he doesn't complain." Jane decided a half lie wouldn't hurt.

The boy looked at the glass for a moment, then swallowed the rest without further complaint. "Uncle Edward was coming to get me, wasn't he? I don't remember anything more. What happened after that."

"Yes, he was. He saved you from the bull, but not before it knocked you down."

"Did the bull knock Uncle Edward down, too?"

"Yes."

"Did it break his arm?"

"No, but its horn wounded him in the side."

The boy's lower lip trembled. "Will he be all right?"

Jane forced a smile. "Yes, I'm sure he will."

Peter hung his head. "Are you very angry with me?" he asked in a tremulous voice. "I know what I did was wrong but . . ."

Jane pulled him close. "Little lambkin, I'm not angry—I'm very happy that you are all right."

He snuggled closer to her. For a few moments she sat silent, stroking his hair. Then she sent Mary to the kitchen for a bowl of porridge. Peter managed to eat half of it before his eyes began to droop—the laudanum was taking effect. Jane tucked the covers around him, took the candle from the night table, and motioned the maid to follow her into the hall.

"I don't think it's necessary to sit up with him anymore," she told the tired girl. "I shall check on him throughout the night—it is night, isn't it?"

"It's past ten in the evening. But, miss, surely you should be getting some sleep, too. We're all afraid you are wearing yourself to the bone. You've not had a proper . . ."

"Yes, I will, thank you." She cut off the girl's protests. "You may bring some breakfast for Peter and perhaps then I will lie down for a bit."

"Well, if you're sure . . ."

"Good night, Mary."

Jane returned to Saybrook's room. His condition had not changed. His breathing was harsh and ragged. When she felt his forehead, it was still hot, but it did seem that the fever had abated slightly. She hoped it wasn't just her imagination.

She placed the candle down and picked up the book she had been reading at odd moments throughout the past few days. How she would manage to keep her eyes open was beyond her, but she must. She opened the slim volume to where her marker lay. It was one of her favorite books, Byron's *The Corsair.* Saybrook had teased her about her liking for Lord Byron, she remembered with a tiny smile. She shot a glance at his chiseled features and watched how the candlelight flickered off the high cheekbones, straight nose, and sensuous lips. She forced her eyes back to the page and let the romantic poetry overwhelm her thoughts.

It was well past midnight when she put the slim leather-bound book aside and rose stiffly from the chair. Every bone ached with weariness and she looked at the large shadowed bed with longing. Rubbing at her temples, it took her a few moments to realize that something seemed different. Saybrook's sleeping suddenly sounded more restful, his breathing more normal. A touch to his brow confirmed that the fever had indeed gone.

"Thank God," she whispered to herself as her eyes brimmed over with tears of gratitude. Her hand slipped down to his and squeezed it gently. It was more than a few minutes before she could bring herself to move from his side. Soon she would not be needed in the sickroom. Then what? It did not bear thinking about in her tired state. Taking up her candle, she went to look in on Peter.

The boy was sleeping peacefully, helped, no doubt, by the influence of the laudanum. There was little for her to do, but she was loath to return to Saybrook's room just yet. A small pile of freshly laundered shirts lay on the mahogany dresser in the far corner of the room. Mary must have forgotten them, so Jane moved to put them away in one of the drawers.

The flicker of another candle caught her eye. She turned, expecting Mrs. Fairchild but instead the figure of the marquess appeared in the doorway. He looked every bit as piratical as the hero in the epic poem she had been reading. His long hair was tangled, a dark stubble covered his chin, and his linen shirt hung open, revealing his bare chest. The fever had left hollows under his cheeks and though his eyes appeared sunken, they were as green as ever. He seemed unaware of her presence. With slow, shuffling steps he moved toward Peter.

Jane almost spoke out, but something held her back. She watched as Saybrook slowly sat on the edge of the bed. His hand ran lightly over Peter's cheek, then he gathered the boy in his arms, taking great care not to jostle the splint, and hugged him tight to his chest. He remained holding the boy in an embrace for some time. Then, brushing a kiss to the boy's forehead, he lay Peter back down and made to rise.

The effort caused his lips to compress with pain. His hand gripped one of the bedposts as he stood unsteadily on his feet.

"Miss Langley," he whispered hoarsely, not wanting to look at her. "I regret that I must ask what is no doubt an odious task of you—but without your assistance I fear I shall not be able to return to my chamber."

Jane wiped away the tears the poignant scene had brought to her eyes and moved quietly to his side. "Steady, sir. If you just put your arm around my shoulder . . ." She in turn slipped hers around his waist. "Now, rest some of your weight on me."

In that manner they were able to slowly cross the hall. With a repressed groan, Saybrook sank onto his bed. His shirt was damp from the effort.

"Please, sir, you must not try to walk yet or you'll bring back the fever," she said as she helped lift his legs onto the bed and pulled the coverlet over them. "You have been very ill . . ."

"Peter—how is Peter?"

"He is going to be fine."

Saybrook let out his breath. "And how long have I been unconscious?"

"Over three days."

"Three days," he muttered. "I . . ." He turned his head and for the first time took in her rumpled clothes and drawn face. "Surely Hastings could have hired a nurse," he exclaimed. "It is not right that you have been forced . . ." He let out an involuntary gasp as Jane felt at his wound.

"The dressing must be changed, sir. If you will just lie still."

Saybrook fell silent. By the clenching of his jaw, Jane could see he was in terrible pain. Hurriedly she cut away the linen bandage and applied the salve as gently as she could. Even so, she could hear a sharp intake of breath.

"I'm sorry," she whispered.

To rewrap the bandage she had to reach around his back, bringing her own body so close to his that she could feel its heat, feel his breath on her cheek. It was all she could do to keep from imitating his own gesture toward Peter.

A small groan escaped his lips.

"Are you in terrible pain, my lord?" She reached for the glass on the night table. "You must try to drink some of this."

His eyes had been closed. At her words they opened slowly and Jane saw they were a bit glazed. He gave a short, bitter laugh. She feared he was slipping back into delirium.

"In pain, my dear Miss Langley? Shall I tell you what pain is?"

She pressed the glass to his lips and was relieved to see he took a few swallows before continuing.

"My mother died when I was fourteen. She had encouraged my interests in the piano and drawing against my father's grumbling that it wasn't manly. After she was gone, he became determined to change me—perhaps in looking back now, it was because I reminded him too much of her, for indeed he did at least love her. She was a remarkable lady. Beautiful, witty, intelligent, and strong enough to moderate my father's rash temper.

On her death, he became . . . angry. With the world, with me."

Saybrook stopped to take a few breaths. He seemed to have forgotten Jane's presence. His eyes had closed again, and it was as if he were speaking to himself as he continued on in barely a whisper.

"My sister was a number of years older than I and had already married and moved to Yorkshire, so I was the only one at home. I begged him to send me away to school, but he refused, saying he would make a man of me before he allowed me to disgrace the family name.

"I learned to ride and hunt and manage the estate well, but I also learned to hate my father. He had become a hard, unforgiving man. If he caught me playing the piano, or with a sketchpad or a book he would beat me.

"Naturally I took to avoiding his presence. I found solace elsewhere." Saybrook's lips compressed. There was such a long silence that Jane feared he had dropped into unconsciousness. But after a heavy sigh, he went on. "There was a tenant family whose daughter had been allowed to get some schooling in the village. We were of the same age, and during my rides around the estate we chanced to talk a few times. I discovered that she loved books, too, and hungered to learn more. I took to lending her some. Then we began to meet—to read, to talk. Her name was Elizabeth. We became . . . friends.

"When my father finally realized he could not beat me into submission, he relented and allowed me to go up to Oxford. It was like a whole new world had opened up for me. I reveled in the studying and had no interest in going with my peers to London to cut a swath in Society. I fear I was rather serious—and rather naive.

"I spent my free time back here, to be with Elizabeth. I was so young in many ways—she was the only person who seemed to understand me. We believed we were in love. I wanted to marry her."

He gave another harsh laugh, low and barely audible. "You can imagine my father's reaction. I was not of age—why I thought he would understand . . . We would have to wait until I attained my majority.

"But then Elizabeth found she was with child. I renewed my arguments with my father, begging to be allowed to do the honorable thing. He merely laughed at me and said I was finally acting like a man—one bedded the neighborhood girls for sport, one didn't marry them. I think it was the first time he had ever approved of me.

"I threatened to run off to Gretna Green if he didn't give in, and he must have finally believed I was serious." Saybrook hesitated, his face looking even more tortured. "The next day Elizabeth was gone, a note in her hand informing me that she hated me for ruining her and that she never wanted to lay eyes on me again. Callow youth that I was, I believed it! I didn't blame her for thinking ill of me.

"Her parents said she had gone to stay with relatives. They refused to say where. I tried to write, but they would not give me any address nor would they accept a missive to deliver themselves. I was told she was better off if I left her alone . . . I believed it.

"I returned to university feeling bitter and disillusioned, with nothing but contempt for myself. Instead of applying myself to my studies, I threw myself into the kind of debaucheries I had previously shunned. Much of my time was spent in Town, drinking, gambling, and indulging in . . . the attractions of the muslin set. I suppose I sought to give my father what he wanted—with a vengeance. After one particularly bad incident, I was sent down.

"One evening, when my father had made one of his trips to London, I was working at his desk. In looking for some correspondence concerning the sale of some stud horses we were interested in buying, I came across a letter hidden in the back of the drawer. It had been addressed to me at Oxford, and forwarded home. I recognized the hand immediately—it was from Elizabeth, asking why I didn't at least take the time to answer any of her other letters. It begged me to be with her for the birth of our child and to see that some provision would be made for its welfare. I knew her well enough to read the anguish and despair.

"In a rage, I raced to her father's cottage and confronted him. He must have sensed that in my mood I was capable of anything, so he confessed that my father had threatened him and his family with ruin if Elizabeth wasn't sent away from me. She was forced to write the note I received and Father arranged for her to be taken on at my sister's estate—though Sarah never knew the truth. Her father was paid—*paid*—for his silence. He knew that my father had bribed someone at Oxford to see that I received none of her letters.

"I rode all that night, and the next day and night as well. But I was a day too late. She had given birth to a healthy baby boy, yet was so despondent and ashamed that she couldn't face going on. She . . . threw herself from the roof of the manor house."

Saybrook halted to steady his voice. "My sister and her husband had been trying for years to have children. When she learned the truth, she begged me to let her keep the child and raise it as her own. Theirs was a remote estate, with loyal servants who would not gossip. No one would ever know it was not hers.

"I didn't care. In fact, for the next few months it was as if I were living in a daze. I considered putting a period to my own existence, but was too cowardly to do so. Finally, I roused myself enough to go home, telling Sarah to do what she saw fit—I couldn't bear to even look at the child. I confronted my father with what he had done. We had a terrible quarrel and, by God, I struck him—I'll never forget the shock in his eyes as he looked up at me from the floor, a trickle of blood coming from his lip. I swore that I would never see him again, turned on my heel, and left. I never did. He died three years later.

"I threw myself into a dissolute life with even more abandon, but even London seemed too close, too much of a reminder. I went abroad . . ." he trailed off. "You can imagine my shock on hearing of my sister and brother-in-law's deaths, and that they had made me Peter—my son's—guardian. How ironic!" His voice was getting softer, the words less distinct as the laudanum took its effect. "So you see, Miss Langley, you were quite right to take a disgust of me. I am quite beyond the pale, don't you think?"

Jane placed her hand on his arm and bent close by his head. "I think it is a very sad story, sir. And I also think it is time you forgave yourself. Anyone would—most of all Elizabeth."

His face looked bleak. "I don't know if I can."

"Did you . . . love her that much?"

He shook his head slightly. "I was . . . grateful for her friendship. Was it love? I don't know. I fancied it was then, but now I doubt that we would have suited as we grew . . ."

Jane felt an unreasonable spasm of relief. She let her hand find his and held it tightly. "You have nothing to be ashamed of, my lord. You acted honorably and as a gentleman should—it is *you* and not your father who are a credit to your family name."

He tried to say something in reply, but the words were thick, incoherent. Already his breathing had lapsed into the regular rhythm of opium-induced sleep. She moved to pull the covers up over his chest, then impulsively brushed a light kiss to his cheek.

"Enough!" cried Mrs. Fairchild in the morning upon finding Jane slumped in her chair. "Both gentlemen are out of danger now and I'll brook no more argument from you! You will go to your own chamber and sleep, or I shall have James and Charles carry you there!"

Jane was too exhausted to argue. She allowed the older woman to shoo her out of Saybrook's room, and on reaching her own bed, she collapsed without undressing and fell into a deep, deep sleep.

Saybrook awoke in the late afternoon, his head finally feeling clear and lucid. He tried to remember all that had taken place, but the events of the past number of days seemed hazy and confused. He wasn't sure exactly what was real and what had been merely dreams—or nightmares. The pain in his side told him that the accident was no figment of his imagination. He remembered the bull and Peter on the ground . . . But had Miss Langley truly been there in his chamber throughout his ordeal, or had it been just a feverish delusion?

He opened his eyes slowly.

"Oh, Mr. Edward! Thank God the fever has passed!" Mrs. Fairchild put down her knitting and came to hover by his bedside.

"Miss Langley. Is she here?" he said softly.

Mrs. Fairchild shook her head reprovingly. "Now, sir, the poor dear has not been to sleep for four days. Cared for both of you, she did, and wouldn't let anyone else near. Surely you wouldn't wish her disturbed—I can get you whatever you need."

So it hadn't been a dream. She had been there.

"Of course," he murmured. "And Peter?"

The housekeeper smiled. "Our biggest worry will be keeping the lad still in bed so that his arm can mend properly."

"That is good news. If you please, I would like a glass of water." He eased himself higher in bed as Mrs. Fairchild fetched the glass, then began to fuss over the pillows.

"I shall manage on my own, thank you," he said, taking the glass. "There is no need for anyone to hover at my bedside—I have no intention of sticking my spoon in the wall in the near future."

"Well, you may tease me, Mr. Edward, but it was a serious thing, it was. Why, without Miss Langley . . ." She trailed off, confused. "I shall send to Cook for some porridge. You must try to eat."

Saybrook lapsed into deep thought. Miss Langley's behavior was puzzling. He could well understand her concern for Peter, and that her sense of responsibility wouldn't allow her to leave in a crisis. But why had she insisted on nursing him as well, when he well knew her disgust of him. Disgust—nay, hatred. And with good reason.

So why had he imagined the tender touch of her lips? Because he was a fool, he chided himself angrily. A fool and delirious. It made no sense. Too weak to think anymore on it, he fell back into an uneasy sleep.

The fresh breeze still felt like a tonic even though four days had passed since Jane had emerged from the sickroom. She pulled her shawl more closely around her shoulders, but kept walking, reveling in the sound of the leaves rustling and the shrill cries of the starlings flying over the meadows.

Peter's protests at having to remain abed still echoed in her ears, but his restlessness cheered all of them, for it meant there were no lingering aftereffects from the blow to the head. She spent mornings with him, fighting grand battles with his lead soldiers among the myriad folds of his bedclothes or reading aloud from one of the Waverly novels.

Mary, the young maid who had shared in the nursing duties, had shown a marked aptitude for dealing with the boy as well. She came from a large family and loved children. Jane was happy to see that Peter took to her, too. She had already mentioned to Mrs. Fairchild that the girl would make a good substitute until another governess—or tutor—could be found.

Of Saybrook she had seen nothing. She had heard he was recovering remarkably well, and that to Dr. Hastings' consternation he had even been up and about for brief periods of time. But she had made it a point to avoid his room and give the library a wide berth. It was just as well that they didn't have to face each other. . . .

Lost in thought, she turned the corner around a high hedge of yews and nearly tripped over a pair of long legs thrust out into the middle of the path.

"Oh, your pardon," she exclaimed, then fell into confused silence when she looked up at who it was.

Saybrook sat on a stone bench. He was dressed casually, a silk dressing gown over his shirt and trousers, a heavy greatcoat draped over his shoulders for protection from the cool breeze. His face was still pale, accentuating the shade of his eyes, but a touch of color was returning to his cheeks. The stubble was gone and his long hair was combed neatly off his forehead. To her dismay, she felt a stab of excitement at seeing him.

"I'm . . . so sorry, my lord," she faltered. "I didn't know you . . . I hope I haven't jostled you."

"Forgive me for startling you." His words sounded cool and stilted. "The air is refreshing, is it not, after being confined to a sickroom?"

Jane nodded, not daring to meet his eyes. Saybrook's hands rested on the chased silver knob of an ebony cane and they tightened imperceptibly.

"I am in your debt, Miss Langley," he continued stiffly, "for your competence and fortitude in caring for Peter—and myself, though I know how unpleasant it must have been for you."

"I was merely doing what was right, sir." Her words sounded horribly trite to her own ears.

"Yes, I know what a refined sense of duty and responsibility you have. Though why you felt it was due . . ." He let it trail off.

Jane made no reply.

"Well." It sounded like a dismissal and Jane began to move away, still not looking at his face.

"A moment, if you please."

She halted.

"I should like to know, that is, I was delirious at times, I believe, and don't recall what was dream and what was . . ." He hesitated. "I mean to say . . ."

Jane looked up at him. "If you mean to ask, sir, whether you told me about Elizabeth, and that Peter is indeed your son—yes, you did."

It was Saybrook's turn to look away. His mouth quirked in a humorless smile. "Ah. Well, you see you were quite right to find my company abhorrent. But you, at least, have escaped with your virtue intact."

"I . . ." she began, furrowing her brow. She stopped for a moment. "It is only yourself who judges so harshly," she finished.

He looked surprised and confused. It appeared he was about to speak further when the tramp of boots on gravel announced the arrival of someone else.

"Beg pardon, my lord." William Coachman bobbed his head. "Mrs. Fairchild thought you was out here and I wanted to inform you that Miss Jane"—he glanced in her direction—"has requested the carriage to take her to Hinchley in the morning."

Saybrook's eyes betrayed a flicker of emotion, but his voice was cool. "Of course. Miss Langley has leave to do as she pleases. See to her wishes." He rose slowly from the bench, steadying himself with the cane, and began a labored walk back to the manor house by himself.

Chapter Ten

Jane felt a lurch in her heart as the hired post chaise turned into the magnificent park. The stately chestnut trees lining the drive were just beginning to take on the burnishings of fall and the air was redolent with the last cutting of hay. Every bend, every tree was achingly familiar, yet seemed somehow different. Had it really been only five months that she had been away? It felt like a lifetime, perhaps because she knew she was not the same person who had slipped away in the middle of the night.

The cart crested the hill and Avanlea Hall came into view. It was an imposing sight. The white limestone facade gleamed in the afternoon sun, its well-proportioned lines set off to perfection by the copse of ancient oak and elm that rose to a soaring height behind the formal gardens. Jane took a deep breath. Her reaction to coming home was always the same—how wonderful it looked!

A groom—it was Joseph—was leading a horse toward the main entrance. A large hound padded alongside him, wagging its tail furiously in its eagerness to be off.

"Why, glory be—it's Lady Jane!" he cried as Jane descended from the open cart herself.

The front door flung open and Thomas emerged, dressed impeccably for riding in tight-fitting buckskins, gleaming Hessians, and a snug coat of navy superfine. He froze in midstride and his mouth dropped in astonishment. Then before Jane could utter a word he sprang forward and gathered her up in his arms. "Thank God you are well," he murmured in her ear as he spun her around. He relaxed his embrace and held her at arm's length. "Let me look at you!" His eyes took in the nondescript, ill-fitting dress, the darkened hair twisted in a tight bun. "What the devil . . ." he began, but stopped at the pleading look on her face. "Oh, I daresay I shall hear about it soon enough." His hands kept a tight grasp on her shoulders. "But I should shake you until your teeth rattle! Have you any idea what you have put us through? Not knowing whether you were lying dead in some ditch . . ."

"Please don't ring a peal over my head just yet," she begged. "I am tired. I am hungry . . . Is Papa here?"

"Indeed he is," replied Thomas, throwing one arm over her shoulder. "Forgive me. It's just that I've been so worried about you." He grinned. "And I've found that I missed you for our curricle races—no one else can drive my grays as well!"

She hugged him. "I've missed you, too."

"Well, shall we seek the bear in his den? Or do you wish to change first?"

"I think it would be best to get it over with." She sighed.

The duke was so engrossed with his correspondence that he didn't hear them enter. Jane was shocked to see how much he had aged, how careworn he looked.

Thomas cleared his throat. "Papa, someone wishes to say hello."

"I'm very busy. Tell them to come back at decent visiting hours," groused the duke. Then he looked up.

He half rose in his chair, then fell back, clutching at the arms until his knuckles turned white. A wave of emotion washed over his face, and it took him a moment to compose himself. "Well, missy. So you have seen fit to come back to us?" His tone was gruff but there were tears in his eyes.

"Oh, Papa." She rushed to his side and threw her arms around him. "I'm sorry," she whispered.

He stroked her hair over and over. "So am I."

Jane reined Midnight to a halt at the crest of the ridge. Her face was tinged a rosy color from the brisk gallop in the crisp morning air and puffs of vapor followed each breath. The big horse stamped at the ground, impatient to be off again, but Jane lingered, taking in the view of the freshly mown field and the stretches of forest already turning a rich autumnal hue.

"Oh, how wonderful to be back at Avanlea." She sighed, though deep down she knew a twinge of sadness kept her joy from being complete.

Thomas had halted beside her. "So, when am I to hear the full story? Just where did you sojourn over these past months?"

She shook her head as she stroked Midnight's mane. "Not now. Maybe later . . ."

"You've always confided in me about everything," he exclaimed, a hurt look in his eye. "Every adventure, every childish prank—"

"Perhaps I have changed. Perhaps I am not a child anymore."

He regarded her sharply. "Very well." He gathered his reins. "Are you, by any chance, in love?"

"Whatever do you mean!" she cried as he prepared to ride off. "What makes you . . ."

"Oh come now, do you take me for such an addlepated fellow? I know you better than anyone! You're right—you have changed. You stare into the fire sadly when you think no one is watching. You have to be spo-

ken to twice to catch your attention—your thoughts are
far from here."

She blushed and hung her head, unable to answer.

"You can talk to me, you know. I won't breathe a
word to anyone—especially Papa," he continued. "Is
it . . . an impossible match? Or is he—God forbid—married?" He cleared his throat. "I hope you haven't been
rash enough . . ."

Her head shot up. "Thomas! How could you think
such a thing!"

It was his turn to color. "I only . . . I didn't . . ." he
stammered. "Dash it all, I'm sorry!"

Jane reached over and patted his arm. "Thank you, I
know you mean well. But there is nothing for you to
do."

"If it is an unequal match, perhaps I can talk to Papa
for you. Despite what has happened, he only wants for
you to be happy, as do I. If he truly felt the two of you
would suit, I think he would give his blessing, despite a
difference in rank or fortune. I just hope," he added,
"that it is not a groom or footman. That may be beyond
even my powers of persuasion."

Jane smiled in spite of herself. "You have changed,
too. I hadn't realized I had such a protective big
brother—you are usually the one encouraging me to land
in the suds."

"A country curate?" he probed, refusing to be distracted.

"There is *nothing* to talk to Papa about. There is no
match, intended or otherwise. Please forget about where
I have been. It is what I intend to do. And now, I
promised Nanna I'd bring her some of Mrs. Hawley's
horehound drops." With that she spurred her mount toward her old nurse's cottage, leaving her brother to can-

ter back to the manor house on his own, a pensive look on his face.

The duke regarded his two children over a glass of vintage port. The two of them were sitting side by side on one of the drawing room couches, laughing over the latest fashions in the *London Gazette*.

"Pray, do not tell me that Althea Westcott appeared at Almack's in *that!*" Jane laughed. "Why, Lady Jersey must have had an attack of vapors."

It did him good to see his daughter in such a lighthearted mood. She had seemed much more serious since her return, so much so that he was concerned. She still would not tell him anything of her time away—what had happened to make her change so? It was a mystery to him. He took a swallow of his drink.

"Jane, you must look to having some new dresses made for yourself. Especially a ball gown."

"A ball gown!" exclaimed both of them in unison. "Why, whatever for," added Jane. "Surely you cannot be thinking of going to Town during hunting season?"

"Your aunt has been pestering me to throw a ball to announce Annabelle's engagement. With you away I wouldn't consider it, but now, well, I think it might enliven the place, don't you agree?" Though it would certainly please his sister, it was his daughter the duke was concerned about. A grand party of young people might be just the thing to bring back her former high spirits.

"How nice," answered Jane without enthusiasm.

"A splendid idea!" added Thomas, with considerable more élan than his sister. "It can be dashed dull here in the country."

"Especially if Miss Livesey and her mamma spend all their time in Town," said Jane with a flicker of a smile.

Thomas rolled his eyes. "Good Lord, that was last spring! Though I admit I would not be averse to having Miss Weston and her family included in the invitations."

Jane laughed aloud. "Why, Thomas, I seem to remember that you thought her a shrinking violet and put a frog in her sewing basket to give her a fright when we visited Overleigh some years ago."

Her brother stiffened. "I should appreciate it if you would not remind her of such childish pranks," he muttered.

The teasing interplay suddenly reminded her of other recent evenings. She rose. "I think I shall leave you two to your port and retire. I'm feeling a bit fatigued."

Her father got up. Motioning to Thomas to remain, he followed his daughter to the door. "I shall see you up, my dear. I, too, am feeling a bit fagged."

As they climbed the broad staircase, the duke studied his daughter's profile in the flickering candlelight. "Missy," he began hesitantly, "is everything all right? I have not wanted to press you, but I cannot help but notice that you seem blue-deviled—you haven't been your old self since coming home." He put a hand on her arm. "And I fear that you may feel you cannot talk to me anymore since—dash it, that damned aunt of yours. I never should have listened to her! I promise you I shall never try to force you into a match you don't wish. I . . . I was wrong."

Jane paused in front of her door and patted his hand. "And so was I, Papa. I know you meant well. If I had more of Mamma's temperament, it would have rubbed along fine. But unfortunately I am much too much like you." She planted a kiss on his cheek. "You mustn't worry about me. You see, I am *not* my old self. I think, perhaps, I have grown up." With that she entered her room, leaving her father to stare after her thoughtfully.

* * *

"May I remind you I am not up for sale at Tattersall's," hissed Saybrook through gritted teeth.

Dr. Hastings finished his proddings and looked up with a slightly reproachful look on his face. "My lord, I'm sorry for causing you any discomfort, but one cannot be too careful. Especially," he added pointedly, "when one's patient refuses to rest properly . . ."

"Hellishly boring to lie abed," muttered Saybrook as he buttoned his shirt.

"Well, despite your efforts to the contrary, you seem to have healed quite nicely."

"Due in no small measure to your skills, Hastings, for which I thank you. And for Peter, too."

The doctor forbore to add that much of the real credit should go to Miss Langley. He was aware that she had departed, and though surprised and curious as to why, he had too much sense to bring up her name. Instead he merely gave a brief nod of acknowledgement. "The lad is right as rain. The bone has mended nicely and there appears to be no lasting damage. Of course he should still keep it in a sling and be kept quiet for the next few days."

Saybrook gave a short laugh. "That will be a miracle to manage. Bed rest suits him even less than it does me. And Mary doesn't have the influence of . . ." He stopped and Dr. Hastings thought he detected a shadow of sadness cross the marquess's face.

Saybrook changed the subject abruptly. "Am I permitted to travel?"

The doctor's brow furrowed in concern. "Is it necessary, sir? It concerns me that you seem intent on jeopardizing your health."

"I have a very pressing matter."

"Well, I would strongly urge against riding. A well-sprung carriage, with the trip done in slow stages . . ."

He shook his head. "It will be very fatiguing at this point, which I don't like. But I suppose it can be done without ill effect."

"Thank you, Doctor. I shall see you out." Saybrook rose stiffly and walked toward the door of his bedchamber. Hastings followed. "Mind you," he admonished, "you must take it slowly, with plenty of rest, or I'll not vouch for your health."

Saybrook nodded. "I shall take full responsibility for my actions."

That night he sat before the fire, once again mulling over a neatly folded piece of paper. William Coachman had done his job well. She had taken a coach from Turnbridge Wells to Finchley. From there, another one to Hartsdale. A hired post chaise had completed the journey. A slight smile came to his lips. A country squire, she had said. Indeed! It was no wonder that her bearing was so different from that of any other country miss, having spent her childhood under the eye of the Duke of Avanlea! William had made discreet inquiries and had learned that yes, a Langley family was one of the duke's tenants, and that their daughter had been childhood friends with the duke's only daughter, a grand heiress in her own right.

Saybrook looked up from William's notes. The minx! Why, he should take her over his knee again for spinning such a Banbury tale. He thought of the look of indignation that would flare in her eyes if he did and smiled again—how he missed her! Then he caught himself. Would it be indignation or some stronger emotion? What would she think if he appeared in her life again? Surely she must hold him in contempt, and yet . . .

He shook his head. Whatever she felt, he had made up his mind. He would not be shaken in his resolve to make sure she was all right. Tomorrow he would leave for

Avanlea. He would speak to the duke himself about using his influence with Jane's father to insure that she not be forced into marriage, for surely His Grace, if he knew, wouldn't want such a thing for his daughter's childhood friend.

Saybrook gazed into the fire. He would also contrive to put Jane in possession of enough funds that she would not have to go into service again. The mere idea of some gentleman casting a designing look at her set his teeth on edge. Perhaps it could be a bequest from a long-lost relative, or—no matter, he would think of something.

He must also see her one last time to explain he had never intended anything improper, had never meant to insult her integrity or virtue. Somehow, it was terribly important that she know, regardless of how difficult the words would be. More than once he had tried to tell her before she left, but his emotions had been buried away for so long that he couldn't seem to bring them forth. A sigh escaped his lips as he put down his glass and made to retire for the night.

Peter sat at the top of the stairs and stared balefully at the trunk sitting near the door. "You're leaving," he said without looking up as Saybrook came down the hallway.

"Only for a short trip, imp."

The boy hunched his shoulders. "No! You'll be just like Miss Jane and go away and never come back." He was fighting to keep a sob from breaking his voice.

Saybrook reached down and scooped Peter into his arms. "Look at me, Peter."

A small, tearstained face turned to him, the lower lip trembling slightly.

"I promise you I shall be back, and soon." He ruffled the boy's hair. "As if I could leave you, brat," he added in a husky whisper.

Peter put his good arm around Saybrook's neck and snuffled. "But I'll miss you, Uncle Edward. I don't want you to go!"

Saybrook sighed in frustration. The poor lad. The last few weeks had been very hard for him as well. There was suddenly the sound of running feet and the rustle of skirts. He turned around.

"Oh, your lordship," said Mary breathlessly. "I've been looking for Master Peter everywhere! Forgive me for allowing him to bother you." The girl was twisting her hands nervously. "I don't know how he manages to slip away . . ."

"Never mind," interrupted the marquess. "Be so good as to pack a valise of Peter's things. He shall be accompanying me."

The boy gave a squeal of delight.

"My lord, will you be wanting me to pack as well?" Mary was totally flustered at the idea. "Certainly you'll be needing someone to look after him."

"That will not be necessary."

The girl appeared uncertain. "Begging your pardon, sir, but who'll dress him and feed him and—it's not fitting that you should . . ."

"I believe that since Briarly is capable of keeping me up to snuff, he should be up to the task of dressing a seven-year-old. And Peter has already proven to me he is perfectly capable of dining in a civilized manner. We shall manage quite well." He put the boy down. "Now go along with Mary and get ready. We've delayed leaving long enough."

"Where are we going?" called Peter as Saybrook started down the stairs.

"You'll see soon enough, imp."

* * *

Jane ran her hand over the exquisite fabric of her new ball gown. Madame Jeannette, the local seamstress, was considered as talented with a needle as any of the top modistes in London, and she prided herself on being au courant on the very latest styles. Her current creation did nothing to diminish her sterling reputation. The dress was of a pale blue watered silk that complemented the color of Jane's eyes and the hue of her hair, golden once again now that she had ceased rinsing it in walnut leaves. The bodice was cut low enough to reveal her creamy shoulders without being improper for a girl of her years, and the fitted waist and deftly set skirts set off her slender figure to perfection. A simple white sarcenet overskirt and a minimum of darker blue ribbons threaded at the hem were all the embellishments that were needed. Her abigail had been in raptures when it had arrived earlier in the day, declaring that Jane would be the belle of the ball. And even Jane had to admit that it looked rather good on her.

The recollection of her reflection in the mirror brought a small smile to her face. Her aunt and cousin would be less than pleased, and though she cared not a whit for upstaging her relation, it was nice to be able to look attractive again. What a dowd she had been forced to be at Highwood—she couldn't help but wonder what the marquess would think of . . .

A knock on her door interrupted her thoughts. Thomas flung it open without waiting for an answer. "Still admiring yourself in the glass?" he teased, tapping his riding crop impatiently against his booted calf. "You promised to ride out with me to look at the new mill! Have you forgotten, or are you mesmerized by the sight of such perfection?"

"Don't be a goose," she retorted, though she colored slightly. "I'm sorry, I was woolgathering for a moment.

I'll be down in a trice—Sarah has already laid out my habit."

"Well hurry, then. The horses are saddled and waiting below."

The two of them were off not more than ten minutes later. With spirited mounts beneath them, eager for a rousing gallop, they quickly left the winding drive and cut out across the rolling meadows in the direction of the river. So they missed seeing the smart carriage pulled by a perfectly matched set of bays pull into the entrance of Avanlea Park.

Chapter Eleven

William Coachman pulled the horses to a halt in the middle of the large courtyard and a young groom immediately ran to their head while another appeared to open the door of the coach.

"Peter, you must wait here with Briarly and William while I speak with the duke," said Saybrook before he descended. He still had not told Peter whom they were seeking to visit. There would be time enough for that when plans were certain.

A stately butler, gray with age yet erect as a soldier, opened the massive oak door. "Yes?" he intoned with the questioning assurance of an old family retainer. Taking in the polished carriage with its crest on the door and its well-matched team, then the tall, handsome gentleman before him with a quick, appraising glance, his bearing seemed to relax slightly. But the gaze he turned on the marquess was still forbidding.

Undaunted, Saybrook placed his card on the silver tray that was held out toward him. "Please convey my apologies for arriving unannounced, and ask the duke if he will see me on a most pressing matter."

The butler bowed slightly and motioned him to come in. "If you will wait in here, my lord, I will see if His Grace is at home."

Saybrook glanced around at the quiet splendor of the room, taking in its rich appointments and elegant furniture. The duke, he noted, was a man of taste, with a purse to indulge his appreciation for quality. Light flooded in through soaring arched windows and glinted off a grand piano. He walked over to the instrument and ran his hand over the polished wood. There was a sudden catch in his breath when he saw the sheet music on the stand. It was a Mozart sonata, the same one that Jane had been striving to learn. . . .

"The duke will see you now."

Saybrook turned quickly and followed the butler out of the room.

The Duke of Avanlea leaned back in his chair and looked curiously at the engraved card before him. Saybrook. He knew his father vaguely, but had never met the present marquess. Not that he hadn't heard rumors. There had been whispers of a scandal concerning a married viscountess, then a widowed baroness, as well as talk of a general dissolute life. Yet others had said the young lord was a sober, serious man. The duke had had little chance to judge for himself, seeing as the marquess had spent most of the past few years on the Continent. What "urgent" matter could Lord Saybrook possibly have to talk to him about? Could Thomas have gotten under the hatches and given him vowels for a gambling debt that he couldn't pay off with his quarterly allowance?

Grimshaw knocked softly, then opened the door to admit the visitor. The duke was immediately struck by the natural grace of Saybrook's bearing, despite a slight limp. It was rare in a man that tall and powerfully built. He was dressed plainly yet elegantly in buff breeches and a dark waistcoat and jacket that bespoke Weston's hand. His cravat was simply tied and no fobs or chains dangled from his middle. The effect was more striking than any of the fripperies sported by the Pinks of the *ton*. The duke looked up into the marquess's face, noting the firm chiseled mouth, high cheekbones, and piercing eyes of indeterminate blue green. The long, dark hair accentuated a firm jaw, one that hinted at an equally firm will. He found himself thinking he could well believe the young lord had a reputation with the ladies.

His eyebrows raised in question. "Lord Saybrook, I have not had the pleasure . . ." He started to rise, but the marquess motioned for him to remain seated.

"Please do not rise on my account, Your Grace. And once again, accept my apologies for intruding upon you without warning."

The duke smiled. "I admit to having my curiosity piqued, sir, for I cannot imagine what matter of yours it is that can concern me—except if my son has . . ."

"No, it is nothing like that," replied Saybrook quickly. He remained standing, even though the duke had waved for him to take a chair. A slight cough indicated how unsure he was as to how to go on. "Your Grace," he finally said, "I believe you have a tenant family of long-standing on your lands by the name of Langley."

Avanlea nodded, even more mystified than before. "Yes. A good man. Both his father and grandfather have worked these lands."

"And the daughter—the daughter grew up with yours, and they formed a fast friendship, despite their difference of rank."

"Yes. Jane and Mary are best of friends."

Saybrook paused. "Jane Langley has served the past number of months as governess to my ward . . ."

"What!" gasped the duke. "What did you say?"

"Jane Langley has been governess to my ward," he repeated. "Though she has recently left my employ, I wish to express my . . . gratitude for all she has done for Peter."

Avanlea made as if to speak, then caught himself. "Go on," was all he uttered.

"Miss Langley has told me that one of the reasons she went into service was that her father meant to force her into a match she did not want." Saybrook fixed a cool look on the duke. "I am sure that, for the sake of your daughter and her feelings, you would not wish such a thing. I would like to ask you to speak to her father—as we both know, the influence of a title can be most persuasive."

The duke stared at him mutely. Nonplussed, he continued. "I would also like your assistance in contriving to make a settlement on Jane so that she does not have to go into service again. She is too spirited a girl to have to endure that."

"On that you have the right of it," said Avanlea. He eyed Saybrook sharply. It was a stare that normally intimidated the person under scrutiny, but the marquess looked back at him coolly, calmly. "Sir," he barked suddenly, "why such interest in a governess? Have you bedded the girl and now wish to buy the family's silence?"

Saybrook went pale, but replied calmly. "A gentleman does not discuss a lady's reputation with another man."

The duke's eyes flashed angrily, and to Saybrook there was an odd familiarity. "What the Devil," began the duke, then trailed off. "I cannot argue with you on that account, sir," he continued ruefully. "But you must understand that I have . . . fatherly feelings for Jane. I am most concerned for her well-being."

"I understand, Your Grace." Saybrook looked at him unwaveringly. "In light of that, let me only say that a father would have no cause for concern."

A sigh of relief escaped the duke's lips.

"I would also ask your leave to speak with Miss Langley." In answer to the duke's questioning look he added, "It is only proper that I seek to inform you as to my intentions regarding someone on your estate."

"But not my permission?" Avanlea permitted himself a slight smile. He rather liked the cool demeanor and quiet purpose of the gentleman before him. A strength of character was certainly evident—and he appeared neither dissolute nor a rake.

Saybrook merely inclined his head slightly but remained silent.

Another question occurred to Avanlea. "Why did Miss Langley leave your employ?"

A long silence followed. "That is something that concerns Miss Langley and myself, Your Grace."

The duke leaned back in his chair and gazed out the library window, deep in thought. "I shall arrange for you to see Jane," he finally announced. "In the meantime, I invite you to pass the night here. You must be weary from your journey, and my son and daughter would be happy to have another face at dinner, I'm sure."

Saybrook bowed. "I thank Your Grace, but I do not wish to impose any further. You see, my ward is accompanying me."

"How old is your ward?"

"Seven years old."

"Rather odd," remarked the duke.

"Peter has been taking Miss Langley's departure hard—he was quite attached to her. Given the circumstances, it would have been rather heartless to abandon him. Until recently I have spent little time at my estate, and he . . . feared I was leaving him, too."

Again Avanlea was struck by Saybrook's sentiments. They were hardly those of a libertine or jaded buck.

"The nursery here is quite cheerful, and one of my kitchen maids is quite used to helping out with my niece's brood when they visit. She would be quite happy to see to your ward's needs."

Saybrook took in a deep breath. His side was beginning to ache something fierce, and for a moment he felt a wave of dizziness.

"Are you all right, sir?" The duke rose in concern.

Saybrook held up his hand. "'Tis nothing. A recent accident has left me a trifle weak at times."

"In that case, I won't hear of your leaving," broke in the duke as he rang for his butler.

Saybrook steadied himself with the back of a chair. "Thank you, sir. Perhaps it would be best if I take advantage of your generous offer."

The duke gave the necessary instructions to Grimsley, then turned back to Saybrook. "I hope you do not mind that we keep country hours here at Avanlea. Please join us at six in the drawing room for a glass of sherry before we go in to dine."

Saybrook bowed and followed the butler from the room.

The duke seated himself once more and stared at the closed door, his hands steepled before him on the massive desk. He considered himself a shrewd judge of character and there was much that impressed—and intrigued—him about the Marquess of Saybrook. Here he sensed a will as strong as his own! He pursed his lips thoughtfully. It should be an interesting evening.

* * *

A short nap had erased the fatigue of the journey, and a hot bath had left him feeling much refreshed. As Saybrook shrugged into his evening coat, he found himself looking forward to the evening. Normally he preferred his solitude, but the chance to meet a dear friend of Jane's had excited his curiosity. And though he hadn't known what to expect, he found himself rather liking the gruff old lord. Saybrook smiled to himself. The duke's concern for Jane was most evident, and he supposed that was what disposed him in Avanlea's favor.

He paused as he began to tie his cravat. The duke had been quick with his hospitality. He had a daughter who, if of an age with Jane, had been out for a Season and was still unmarried. A horrible thought crossed his mind. He began to envision a squat, squint-eyed young lady— yes, it would be just like Jane to adopt someone like that! The duke couldn't be thinking of . . . Suddenly he relaxed and laughed at his own fears. With her rank and dowry, the Miss Stanhope could be a veritable harridan and she would not lack for offers. Breathing a sigh of relief, he straightened the folds of his neckcloth and rang for a footman. It should be an interesting evening.

After looking in on Peter and finding him comfortably settled, Saybrook presented himself at the drawing room door precisely at six. The duke greeted him and as they exchanged pleasantries, Saybrook noted that the two young people were at the far end of the room by the fireplace, deeply engrossed in their own conversation.

They had not seen his entrance, for their backs were to him. For a moment, he had a chance to study their appearances. The young man was nearly as tall as himself, slim but solid, with well-muscled legs that his expertly tailored clothes showed off to perfection. Weston, no doubt. And no doubt that the heir to Avanlea could cut quite a swath in Town if he chose.

But it was the lady who caught his attention. He nearly laughed aloud thinking of the mental image he had formed beforehand—it couldn't have been further from the truth. She was tall and elegantly slender. Masses of honey-colored hair were dressed in a most becoming style, with just a few loose tendrils drifting down a long and graceful neck. The color of her gown brought out the rich gold of her hair, while the expert cut flattered an already lovely figure. Saybrook felt an involuntary surge of admiration. She was a Diamond of the First Water, for he had no doubt that picture would be no less lovely when she turned around. What a ninnyhammer he had been! Yet it was strange, there was an odd familiarity about her . . .

The duke took his arm and moved toward the fire. "Come now, you two. Don't put me to the blush with your manners. Our guest has arrived. Sir," he said to Saybrook, "may I present my son Thomas, Viscount Roxbury."

The young man turned. His face was handsome, with eyes as blue as his father's, and he smiled politely as he sketched a quick bow. Saybrook felt a slight shock as he realized that the young man so resembled Jane that they could have been twins, except for the blond hair. Now it was easy to guess at why the duke had a fatherly regard for Miss Langley—clearly his interest in his tenants had gone beyond sowing merely wheat.

"And may I present my daughter."

Saybrook's mouth dropped in astonishment as the young lady turned to face him.

"I believe you are acquainted with Jane," continued the duke blandly. "However I fear you are confused as to her last name. It is Stanhope, not Langley."

She looked exactly as she had in his dreams, when he had imagined her dressed in expensive silks and fitted gowns rather than her own drab, ill-fitting garments. Instead of a high-buttoned neck reaching nearly to her chin, her dress of moss green figured silk exposed a pair of creamy shoulders and enough bosom to take his breath away. The high waist only heightened the awareness of the rounded curves above it while showing off the slim waist and womanly shape beneath it. With the walnut stain gone, her hair resembled nothing like the mousy color it had been at Highwood but shone like burnished gold. Her skin had a milky luminance matched by the simple strand of pearls at her throat.

He stood in stunned silence, his mouth dry, his body rigid.

Jane appeared just as surprised. Her eyes widened in shock and her polite smile changed to a look of disbelief. "You! How did you . . ." she blurted out before she recovered enough to stammer, "How do you do, sir."

Saybrook, barely conscious enough to bow over her extended hand, was saved from having to reply by the entrance of the butler.

"Dinner is served, Your Grace."

The meal was a strained affair. Both Saybrook and Jane answered any direct question put to them in stilted tones but otherwise remained silent. Thomas shot both of them quizzical glances while keeping up a running conversation with his father. The duke jovially discussed the merits of some newly acquired horses, seemingly oblivious to the tension around him. However, despite his feigned nonchalance, he kept a sharp eye on his daughter and their guest. The spark between the two of them was evident during the few times their eyes accidentally met.

"Is your ward comfortably settled in the nursery?" inquired the duke.

"Yes, thank you."

Jane looked up from her plate. "Is Peter here?" she exclaimed.

Saybrook didn't look at her. "Yes."

"Oh, how is he? How is his arm?"

"His arm has mended nicely." Saybrook paused. "He misses you terribly," he added in a low voice.

"Oh." She fought to keep the tears out of her eyes. "As do I," she finished softly.

There was an awkward silence until Thomas finally spoke. "May I ask what is going on here?"

When neither of them answered, the duke cleared his throat. "It appears that Jane has spent the last number of months as governess to Lord Saybrook's ward . . ."

"Good Lord," whispered Thomas, looking at his sister in astonishment.

" . . . representing herself as Jane Langley, a farmer's daughter." He looked reprovingly at his daughter. "Most unfair of you, missy. Do you realize what a potentially disastrous position you placed the marquess in?"

She looked at him, startled.

"Why," continued her father, "if the merest whisper had gotten out, his lordship, as a gentleman, would have been forced to offer for you, regardless of his feelings in the matter."

"I . . . I hadn't thought of that."

"Not to speak of your own reputation!" Avanlea turned to Saybrook, who had turned a shade paler at the duke's words. "I beg your forgiveness for my daughter's actions. I trust you will agree with me that it is best that this matter go no farther than this table."

"Of course. You have my word," said Saybrook.

The duke nodded. "And you mine," he added pointedly.

Thomas in the meantime had recovered from his initial shock. "A governess." He chuckled, ignoring the pleading look from his sister. "Willful, stubborn, impatient, opinionated—I can hardly credit that my dear sister wasn't more trouble than her charge! You don't mean to tell me that she actually obeyed orders without a scene?"

The duke noticed that for the first time a smile, a very faint one, came to the marquess's lips. "Well," he replied softly, "if you discount the time she threatened to take a horsewhip to me . . ."

"She *didn't!*"

Jane's face was nearly crimson as Saybrook nodded in assent. "Indeed she did."

"Good Lord! And you didn't turn her out immediately?" Thomas looked at him in puzzlement. "Why?"

"She was right. I had behaved abominably toward a child, my ward. I do not turn out my people for speaking the truth—though I did request that she express her future opinions of my conduct in a more moderate fashion." There was a slight pause. "And she was an excellent governess—kind, generous, patient, and understanding."

"But what of the times she wasn't right? I know my sister well enough to know she isn't *always* right."

"Most of the time we were able to reach an accord in a rational manner."

"Most?" persisted Thomas, a mischievous grin on his face. "What of the others?"

Saybrook considered the question for a moment. "I believe I only had to spank her once . . ."

Thomas let out a shout of laughter and shook his head in admiration. "By Jove, I'd have paid any amount of blount to see that! Come, Jane, what was your reaction?"

Jane's face was even redder.

"I believe Lady Stanhope would not care to repeat her reaction," answered Saybrook dryly. "The words she spoke would not have led one to believe she was a Lady of Quality."

Thomas's grin grew wider. "I'm afraid I'm well acquainted with my sister's vocabulary."

Jane lifted her chin. "I should hope I am as fair-minded as Lord Saybrook. I acknowledge that in that case he was right—though I, too, asked that he vent his feelings in a more appropriate manner."

"At the time, it *was* the most appropriate manner," muttered Saybrook, much to Thomas's amusement.

The duke decided it was time to change the subject. "I hope, Saybrook, we shall have the pleasure of your company for an extended visit. I look forward to meeting the young lad who has occupied so much of my daughter's attention for the past months."

Saybrook shook his head. "I think not. It would be best if we leave in the morning now that there is no need . . ."

"Surely not!" interrupted the duke. "I'm certain it would do your injury no good to travel again so soon, and I can see that my daughter would be bitterly disappointed in not being able to spend some time with the boy."

Saybrook began to speak.

"Besides," added Avanlea, "we have a ball planned for my niece and are in need of all the gentlemen we can muster. I would take it as a great favor if you would at least stay until then."

"I . . ."

"Please, sir." Jane's voice was nearly inaudible.

The turmoil was evident on Saybrook's face. "I . . ."

"Good!" boomed the duke. "It's settled, then."

Saybrook's lips compressed into a tight smile. "You are most persuasive, Your Grace."

The duke returned the smile. "No, I simply refuse to take no for an answer. Prerogative of rank."

At that moment, the footmen came in to clear the table. As they left, Jane rose, too. "If you will excuse me, I shall leave you gentlemen to your port. I think I will retire early tonight. I . . . feel a bit of a headache."

"Headache," remarked Thomas as he stared at her retreating figure. "Why, she's never had . . ." A quelling look from his father silenced any further words.

"I pray you will also excuse me." Saybrook stood up. "It has been a fatiguing day."

The duke rang for a candle. "Good night to you, sir. Let Grimshaw know if you are in need of anything."

Saybrook made a bow, an inscrutable look on his face. "I believe you have thought of everything, Your Grace." With that, he followed the footman to the door.

Walking to the sideboard, the duke poured himself a large port and held it eye level, a smile on his face as he regarded its rich, ruby color.

"What on earth are you grinning like a Bedlamite for?" demanded his son.

"Oh, I think you shall see soon enough." He took a sip from his glass. "But I wouldn't be young again for all the tea in China."

"Why . . ."

He shook his head in exasperation. "Youthful pride. It makes you young people too blind to see what's in front of your noses."

"You don't mean—why, it's clear they don't even *like* each other!"

The duke started on his way to the drawing room. "Thomas, you disappoint me," he said. "Until now, I would never have considered my heir an utter fool."

Jane pulled her nightgown closer as she sat on the window seat of her chamber, watching the moonlight play off the boxwood hedges and ornamental shade trees.

Drat the man. Just when she was beginning to think she could put him out of her mind, he had to reappear in her life, upsetting her carefully constructed equilibrium. Upon raising her eyes and meeting those familiar sea green ones, upon seeing him standing there looking devastatingly handsome in his evening clothes, it had taken only a second for the foundations to come tumbling down.

How had he found her? And more puzzling, what was he doing here?

She had to blink back tears. Surely he must hold her beneath contempt now that he knew of her lies, her deceit. Surely that was what she had seen in his eyes the few times their glances had crossed during the evening, before he had quickly averted his face. Why, he couldn't even bear looking at her.

It would have been much better if she had encouraged him to go on the morrow. So why had she asked him to stay? She rose and began to pace the room. She had asked him because—Jane caught herself. A sudden realization washed over her. Coward! For months she had been a coward, she who had always prided herself with not being afraid to face anything. She had been afraid of her feelings, afraid of risking not only her precious independence but her heart as well. It was only now that she understood risk was a part of life, and that the rewards were worth far more than youthful pride.

But finally realizing the truth did not make it any easier to know what to do. It was probably too late now to win back his regard. What a mull she had made of things, she who was always so sure she knew best. It was a bitter pill to swallow to realize how bullheaded she had been in not telling Saybrook the truth when she had had a chance. She should have trusted that he would understand. Now . . . She climbed between the covers to ward off the chill that was creeping over her, but she knew that sleep would be a long, long time in coming.

Jane was not the only one pacing the floor of a bed-chamber. Saybrook was also in such an agitated state of mind that he couldn't sleep, despite his physical fatigue. He laughed harshly at himself. What a fool she had played him for. Only a complete gudgeon would not have known that "Jane" was no ordinary country miss. And as her father pointed out, he had also been placed in a scandalous position for both of them, and of scandals he had had enough. Yet despite his hot anger at having been duped, he felt an infinite sadness at the loss of his "Miss Langley." His mouth crooked in an involuntary smile when he pictured her once more in her dreadful gown, her hair twisted in an unattractive bun, her eyes flashing as she argued some point with him.

He forced the image from his mind. She was irrevocably gone. A duke's daughter and a grand heiress. Why, her father—and no doubt Jane herself—would think him a mere fortune hunter intent of taking advantage of the situation if he offered for her now. That he couldn't bear.

An oath escaped him. Why had he allowed himself to be maneuvered into staying here. He should depart at first light, no matter his promises and Peter's disappointment. He should be far enough away where he would be sure of never seeing her again until she was safely married. Perhaps to the Continent again. Wearily, he sank onto the bed and buried his hands in his hair. He could deal with the pain if he didn't have to see her. Oh yes, he was an expert at dealing with pain.

Jane smiled as she watched Peter urge his pony into a gallop as they returned to the stables. The boy was having a wonderful time. If she didn't know him better, she might worry that he was being dreadfully spoiled, what with all the attention from every adult in the house. Why, even her father had been taken with the boy. She had found him showing Peter how to feed the ducks out by the pond. The duke had looked up and with a pointed look had remarked on how lively the place was with brats about.

But Saybrook was another matter. It was as if he were at the other end of the earth. In the two days since his arrival he had barely uttered a word during meals and retired immediately afterward. Unable to ride, he spent most of his time taking long, solitary walks or sequestering himself in the duke's library. Not once had he spoken a direct word to her. In fact, it was obvious he went to great pains to avoid being in her presence.

She felt the sting of tears. What had she expected? As the stables neared, she wiped at her eyes with her sleeve. At least after tomorrow he would be gone and she could at last forget about him.

Thomas was taking Peter to see the kennels for the afternoon, so Jane finally had a few hours to herself. She changed out of her riding habit and picked up a book from her escritoire. Throwing a shawl over her shoulders, she left the room, praying that none of the servants would stop her with some household matter that needed her attention. Slipping out through the French doors of the breakfast room, she hurried down a path behind the formal gardens. Since she was a small girl, she had had a favorite spot, one she always went to when she needed solitude or comfort. It was a small knoll overlooking the lush grazing lands that rolled down to the river. Surrounded on three sides by a thicket of small hemlocks was a weathered wooden bench where she had spent countless hours reading or just watching the light play off the distant water.

She glanced down at the book she was carrying. It was a small leather-bound volume, the same one she had been reading that night in the sickroom at Highwood. How she and Saybrook had once argued over the contents. She had insisted on reading him passages of *The Corsair* to refute his casual remark that Byron was a self-conscious romantic, not a great, passionate poet. He had listened, a sardonic smile on his face, then had admitted that such words might set a woman's heart aflutter—she had nearly thrown the book at him until he could contain his laughter no longer and she had seen he was teasing her. He then allowed that he did admire the poet's fiery soul, though at times he was a trifle melodramatic. Then, to her great surprise, he had insisted that she keep the expensive copy from his library, saying the book suited her "impassioned nature."

Jane reached the glade and settled herself on the bench, drawing her shawl around her. As usual, she wore no bonnet around the estate, for she loved the feeling of the sun on her face, regardless of its detrimental effects on a lady's complexion. Throwing her head back to catch the pale warmth, she closed her eyes for a minute. There was stillness, save for the faint rustle of pine needles in the gentle breeze. So many times she had sought refuge here from life's heartaches. Why, she could remember quite clearly when she thought, at age fourteen, that she would simply die because her father refused to let her join the hunt because she was a girl. She shook her head, able to smile at the old memory. Perhaps time did make things easier to bear. She opened the book and began to read.

Sometime later, the sound of footsteps broke the spell of the words. From her hidden vantage point she watched a figure moving out of the trees into the clearing. Saybrook, too, wore no hat and the breeze ruffled his long dark locks, causing a certain stirring deep within her. He turned and walked toward her, unaware of the bench concealed in the hemlocks. By the time he came around the trees, he was no more than a few feet from where she sat.

His eyes widened with surprise. There was a spark of something else as well before it disappeared in an instant, to be replaced by the cold, distant look that had become too familiar. "Your pardon," he said stiffly. "I had no idea anyone was here." He made as if to turn, but hesitated as he saw the book in her hands.

"Yes," she faltered. "I am indulging my . . . my . . ."

" . . . impassioned nature," he finished, his voice barely above a whisper.

Suddenly the words came pouring out. She didn't dare look at him or stop to think at all, for she knew she wouldn't have the courage to go on if she did.

Saybrook listened in silence, his eyes never leaving her face.

"So you see, my lord," she ended, still keeping her eyes averted from him, "I truly did not mean to deceive you. I was afraid to tell you later on for fear you would . . . hate me."

"*Hate* you?" repeated Saybrook.

"Yes! You told me how you hated the way ladies of the *ton* lied and deceived and manipulated for their own gain!" Her voice was trembling now. "And you made it quite clear that you thought most were like that—but that I was different. I did not want to . . . lose what regard you might have held for me. But I suppose I have shown I am indeed no different, and am deserving of your contempt."

Saybrook muttered an oath. "Miss Lan—Lady Stanhope, I do *not* hate you."

Jane finally dared look at him. "But you have been acting as if you do."

"It is *I* who do not wish to inflict my presence on *you.*"

Her eyes betrayed her confusion. "But why?"

He took a deep breath. "I think you may guess why."

"You mean because Peter is your son?"

He nodded. "That, and because I am worse than an unprincipled rake, having caused the death of . . ."

"No! That is not . . ."

A loud barking interrupted her words, followed by the sound of voices.

"Up this way?" came Peter's shout.

"Yes. I'll lay a wager we find her here. It's her favorite spot."

A large hound burst out of the woods and raced across the glade, planting his muddy paws squarely on Jane's shoulders.

"Oh, down, Memphis," she cried, wishing her brother did not know her so well.

Thomas and the boy were close on the dog's heels.

"Isn't Memphis bang up to the mark!" cried Peter as he ran up to them. "And Thomas says I may have one of his puppies! That is, Uncle Edward, if you agree." He looked up at Saybrook with pleading eyes. "Would you like to go see them? Now?"

Despite his tangled emotions, Saybrook couldn't suppress a harried smile. "Very well, let us go inspect these prized progenies." He let the boy grab his hand. "I suppose Highwood would be sadly lacking without a hound sired by so august a personage as Memphis."

Thomas cocked an eyebrow at his sister as Peter half dragged the marquess away. "I fear my timing has been less than perfect."

Jane made a show of gathering her things. "No," she answered, deliberately misunderstanding him, "it's just about time to change for dinner, isn't it?"

Chapter Twelve

Jane smoothed the rich silk around her knees then fidgeted once more on the stool. "La, Miss Jane. Hold still or I'll never finish your hair." Sarah made a few more deft adjustments then stepped back to admire the effect. "There now, that's perfect. If you aren't the most beautiful lady in the land!"

"Oh, Sarah, stop or you'll turn me into a conceited monster." Jane regarded her own image in the mirror and had to admit she was not displeased. "But you are a magician."

Her maid beamed with pleasure. "As if you'd ever be a monster like your cous . . ."

"Sarah," warned Jane.

"Well, it's the truth." The older woman sniffed. A sly grin crept over her face. "Won't Lady Fisher be mad as a wet cat when she sees you. What I wouldn't give to see it!"

"That's very uncharitable," scolded Jane, but she couldn't repress a smile. Her aunt did her best to make everyone at Avanlea miserable, so she couldn't blame the servants for taking delight at the thought of her comeuppance.

"What a grand evening it should be," continued Sarah. "The ballroom looks like it's right out of one of those fairy tales your nurse used to read to you."

Jane's hands were knotted in her lap. "Yes." She sighed, trying to sound enthusiastic.

"What's this? Blue-deviled on a night like this. For shame!" She shot her charge a shrewd look. "Why I hear that all the young bucks have come up from Town. Lord Astley is at his estate and it's said Lord Hawthorne is staying with him. You'll have no lack of dancing partners."

Jane smiled as she opened her jewelry case.

"And of course there's that handsome lord what's staying here. Devilishly attractive is that one. Quiet he is, and a bit mysterious if I do say so. Surely he'll be there as well."

Jane's fingers fumbled with the catch of her necklace, a double strand of pearls with a starburst pendant of cut sapphires. A knock on the door saved her from having to reply.

"Don't be all evening! The guests will be arriving any moment." Thomas poked his head in the door and gave an appreciative whistle. "You look magnificent, my dear."

"Fustian," she murmured but was secretly glad that he thought she looked good. She snapped the clasp in place and pulled on her kid gloves. As she hurried to the door, she stopped to plant a kiss on her maid's cheek. "Don't bother waiting up for me. I shall tell you all about it in the morning."

Sarah had been right. The ballroom looked absolutely enchanting. Even though Jane had helped supervise the gardeners in arranging the garlands of evergreens and the fragrant flowers from the greenhouses, the glittering of the chandeliers along with the hundreds of snowy candles placed in among the greens brought a special magic to the space. At the far end of the room, on a platform nearly hidden by sheaves of wheat and arrangements of cabbage roses, the musicians began to warm up.

The ballroom was fast filling up with guests. Some of the older gentlemen made no pretense of being interested in dancing and made straight for the card room. A few old dowagers and apprehensive mammas sat grouped together where they could keep their basilisk stares on the dance floor. Jane was relieved that her aunt had insisted on doing the honors with her father in the receiving line. It gave her time to look around and compose her thoughts.

"Welcome back, Lady Jane. I trust your relative is quite recovered." Jane turned to a familiar face, framed by short auburn curls carefully arranged à la Brutus. "I know *we* shall never recover from your absence from the Season," continued the smooth voice as her hand was lifted toward his lips.

She managed a smile. "How kind, Lord Frederick, though I'm sure life was not quite so sadly flat as you hint."

"Oh, it was." He held her hand longer than necessary and she had to restrain the urge to yank it away. At that moment she thought him a conceited prig! Was he so sure of himself that he was oblivious to her lack of particular regard?

He reached for her dance card. "Ah, the rewards of being unfashionably early." He smiled. "I shall claim the first waltz, as well as . . ."

"I'm sorry. I'm promised for the first waltz."

His eyes flickered with annoyance. "I see no name there."

"Nevertheless, it is taken."

"Who . . ." began the young duke, when a group of other gentlemen descended upon them. Jane was saved from further conversation with him as she exchanged greetings with her well-wishers. Within minutes, her card was filled for the evening, Lord Frederick having had to satisfy himself with the supper dance and a later waltz. The music began and she was led out for the opening set of country dances. Her partner, Viscount Stoneleigh, was an old friend who also chided her on her long absence from Society. With a twinkle in his eye, he promised to bring her up to date on all that had happened. Despite his droll observations on the latest *on-dits,* Jane found her attention wandering. Her eyes searched the crowded room. Surely he must be here by now. Unaware of the music, she made a glaring misstep, causing her partner to tread on the toe of her slipper.

"Your pardon!" Stoneleigh apologized, peering at her startled face. "Lady Jane, I fear you haven't heard a word I have been saying!"

Jane blushed guiltily and forced herself to banter with him until the dance ended and he led her back to the group of her admirers.

Her next partner was sent to fetch lemonade, giving her time to look around once more. She caught her breath as she saw Saybrook standing alone, arms crossed, surveying the room. He looked magnificent in his evening clothes. The other lords suddenly seemed like a flock of poppinjays with their striped waistcoats, bright colors, and dangling fobs and seals. Saybrook was dressed entirely in black, save for the snowy cravat at his throat and a single gold signet ring on his finger. He seemed not to notice her at all, his eyes sweeping past her as if she were merely one of the decorative blooms. With a tiny sigh of disappointment she turned back to her partner with an animated smile and feigned a light-hearted gayness.

After yet another dance Jane begged a moment to take a chair. She knew what was coming next. Already the musicians were running through the first few bars of the lilting melody in order to get ready. Resisting the urge to look around yet again, she made herself listen with a smile to the vicar's wife prose on about her weak constitution.

"What sort of mutton-headed fool leaves a Diamond of the First Water sitting out a waltz?" growled Lord Frederick as he bent close to her ear.

"I am quite exhausted. I prefer to sit," she answered quietly.

"Nonsense. I won't allow it."

"Lord Frederick, please. I do not wish to," she said, trying to evade his hand.

He had succeeded in taking hold of her however, and rather than make an unpleasant scene, she rose reluctantly.

"I believe Lady Stanhope is promised for this dance."

The deep voice sent a thrill down Jane's spine.

Lord Frederick turned to face the tall stranger. "Since you, sir have been so rag-mannered as to leave the lady waiting, I believe you have forfeited your right." He glared with a smug expression, confident that such a ringing set-down would send the man slinking away.

"I think not." Saybrook's voice was still low, but with an icy coolness that made Lord Frederick draw back in surprise. Saybrook's hand was already on Jane's elbow and he guided her to the dance floor before the startled duke could say another word. They took their positions silently and the musicians began to play.

Like before, she followed him effortlessly, instinctively. As they floated along with a natural grace that drew admiring glances from the couples around them she was intensely aware of his hand on the small of her back, the heat emanating from the closeness of his body, his earthy, masculine scent. Unconsciously she squeezed his hand. In response he pulled her a fraction of an inch closer. At that, she summoned the courage to look up at him. His eyes were riveted on her face, his expression intent yet inscrutable.

"You . . . you remembered," she managed to say.

"As if I could forget," he murmured in a husky whisper.

Nothing was said for another few moments. Then he spoke again, still in a near whisper. "Let me say that your gown is infinitely more becoming than the one you were wearing last time we danced."

A smile came to her lips and she saw an immediate softening of his features. "Don't remind me of how hideous I must have looked. Thank goodness you are well rid of such a sight."

"You are very wrong. 'Tis a great sadness to me that Miss Langley has disappeared."

"But she hasn't, sir. She is here."

"Is she?"

Before Jane could answer, he tightened his hold on her waist and swept her along at a quickened pace. Her heart was racing, whether from exertion or the sudden wave of emotion, she couldn't tell. She couldn't tell much of anything. The rest of the dance was a blur, and when he released her to lead her back to her next partner she was amazed to find that her legs were steady enough to support her.

There was already a cluster of gentlemen waiting for her return. They eyed Saybrook with expressions that ranged from speculative to downright hostile. Suddenly Jane couldn't bear the idea of anyone else's touch. As Saybrook left her with a slight bow, she turned to Lord Morton, the next name on her list.

"Please excuse me, sir," she said as she fumbled with the fold of her gown. "I seem to have a small tear at my hem that simply must be mended."

Without waiting for a reply she turned and made her way through the crowd. Reaching the hallway, she hurried past the ladies' withdrawing room, praying that no prying tabby would note her strange behavior. The drawing room was empty, lit only by moonlight. As she flung open the French doors and stepped outside a wave of cool air washed over her. It felt good on her flushed cheeks, and she stood still, breathing it in deeply. To her chagrin, she felt tears trickling down her cheeks. She scolded herself for being ridiculous. Why, she seemed to have turned into a veritable watering pot these days. With a loud sniff, she reached to wipe them away.

"Allow me."

Saybrook came around to face her and dabbed gently at her face with a white silk handkerchief. Returning it to his pocket, he slipped off his coat and settled it around her shoulders.

She turned away in confusion. "I . . . I was too warm and just came out for a breath of air. I must be getting back."

He placed a hand on her arm. "A moment longer." He turned her round to face him. "Why are you crying?"

"Why did you come here?" she countered, her jaw thrusting out defiantly. "And I'm *not* crying. The cold air has merely made me tear . . ."

For the first time in ages, Saybrook gave a hearty chuckle. "You are right—my dear, defiant, prickly Miss Langley is still here."

"I'm not prickly," she retorted. "It's just that you bring out . . ." She stopped as he ran the back of his hand down her jawline.

"No," he whispered. "On that I am very wrong."

Suddenly she felt hot all over again.

"Why did you come here?" she repeated.

He was silent for a number of moments. "To see Miss Langley. To ask . . . her forgiveness . . ."

"Sir! The past is done with. There is nothing for which you need forgiveness. You are a good man, a kind, compassionate, honorable man. The past is over. It is time to move on with your life."

"Yes," he mused. "Yes, I have come to that decision as well. And so I came to do properly what I made a terrible mull of the first time I tried it."

Jane's mouth went dry. "What is that?"

His sea green eyes flickered in the pale moonlight. "I was afraid to say what I truly felt," he went on. "Afraid of—no matter. I have come to realize it is infinitely harder to bear hiding one's feelings than it is to risk hurt."

"And perhaps I was afraid to hear it, for all the same reasons." Jane met his gaze. "But . . ." She hesitated. "These past few days you have remained silent. Has something changed?"

"Yes, it has."

Jane felt a rush of sadness, regret. The tears welled up again and she dropped her head. "I see."

"The governess is now a lady of great rank and wealth."

"And that matters because I lied to you," she mumbled.

Saybrook lifted her chin. "For such an intelligent person, you have come up with a most nonsensical notion. It matters because I fear you may think me no better than a fortune hunter or . . ."

"Now it is you who have windmills in your head. As if I could think such a thing! You forget that I already know your faults."

Saybrook's hands moved to her shoulders. The coat slid to the ground. "Lord, what fools we both have been," he whispered as he pulled her close. "Jane, my dearest Jane. I love you beyond reason. Will you marry me?"

"Yes."

"Truly?"

"Most truly, darling. Surely any man less modest would have known I've been head over heels in love with you for an age." Her head was resting on his shoulder and she turned it to look up at him.

His lips came down on hers, tender but full of need. It took but a moment to ignite the smoldering passion in both of them. Saybrook's tongue demanded entry, and she opened wide for him, with a soft moan of desire. He thrust in deeply, drinking the taste of her while she, shy at first, then more boldly, explored him as well.

He released her mouth only to trail his lips along the curve of her neck down to the edge of her gown.

"My darling," he groaned as his hands cupped her breasts. Then he slid a finger inside her bodice, pulling it down to expose the rounded flesh. Jane gave a gasp of pleasure as he took her nipple between his teeth, feeling it harden as he caressed it with his tongue.

"Edward," she moaned, her nails digging through the fine fabric of his shirt to the rippling muscles beneath.

"Say it again, my love," he urged. "Let me hear my name on your lips once more." He began to kiss her other breast.

Jane repeated his name over and over again as she slid her hands down to his buttocks and pulled him tight, so she could feel the hardened ridge of his manhood pressing against her. With another groan, he gently undid her arms and held her away.

"Love, we must wait till our wedding night—and in another moment that will be impossible," he whispered raggedly. The disappointment and desire in her eyes made him smile crookedly as he straightened the front of her gown. "Damnation that your father is a duke and we cannot be married tomorrow by special license. But promise me it will be a short engagement." He bent to kiss her once more. "I'm not sure I can survive much longer in this state."

"As short as can be allowed," she agreed. "You know how a governess must keep furthering her education— and I am quite curious to see what happens from here." As she spoke, she ran her hand along the front of his thigh.

"Hoyden," he said with a groan. "Behave yourself or I shall have to take you over my knee." And he claimed another kiss.

"And you, my lord, remember there is always a horse-whip to keep you in line."

Their muffled laughter floated through the air as Saybrook bent to pick up his coat. "I suppose we had better return." He sighed.

As they reentered the drawing room, a lone figure seated in one of the brocade wing chairs was silhouetted by the moonlight. The duke had his legs stretched out comfortably in front of him, a glass of cognac held in one hand as he contemplated the thick cigar in the other.

"Ah, Saybrook," he drawled. "I believe you were looking for me?"

"As a matter of fact, Your Grace . . ."

"The answer is yes."

Both Jane and Saybrook looked startled.

"Any man with the fortitude to take my daughter over his knee has my wholehearted blessings. So, yes. Yes! Before you change your mind!"

"Father!" cried Jane indignantly.

The duke let out a chuckle. Jane opened her mouth to retort but found herself laughing as well as her father rose and gave her a hug.

"You have chosen much better than I," he murmured in her ear. "I believe you will be very happy." He extended his hand to Saybrook and added, "I believe that an announcement of our own is in order . . . You may wish to retie your cravat. The, er, wind seems to have caused some disarray."

"But, Papa, Aunt Bella will have a fit of vapors if we take the attention from Cousin Annabelle!"

"Quite." A rather satisfied smile spread over the duke's face. "She vastly deserves it, too, for all of her meddling . . ."

"I, for one, would like to embrace the dear lady," interrupted Saybrook.

Jane and her father looked at him as if he were mad. "But, Edward, you can't imagine . . ." began Jane.

"Without her, I would not have met you." He grinned.

"You have a point," conceded the duke. "We shall wait until the end of the evening and let her bask in the attention until then."

"Papa, before we return to the ballroom Edward and I must visit the nursery."

He nodded, smiling broadly. "Of course the lad must know. I shall wait for you here and savor my good fortune." He lit his cigar. "You know, I look forward to seeing Peter here at Avanlea often—along with his brothers and sisters," he added as the two of them left the room.

"Mmmm," said Saybrook, nuzzling close to her ear as they climbed the stairs. "*Lots* of brothers and sisters."

"Edward . . ." Her words were cut off by yet another kiss.

"Very soon."